Sour Worlds
Calamities

Jaymes Bishop

Table of Contents

Prologue: The Vanishing 5
Chapter One: The Gathering 1
Chapter Two: The Warning..............................5
Chapter Three: Entering The Woods............10
Chapter Four: The First Sign..........................15
Chapter Five: Lauren's Dream 20
Chapter Six: The Tangles 24
Chapter Seven: Night of the Tangles..............30
Chapter Eight: The Hunt in Silence 35
Perspective: The Knot.....................................39
Chapter Nine: The Knot's Journey 41
Chapter Ten: Children of the Knot.................45
Chapter Eleven: The Knot's Vision.................49
Chapter Twelve: The First Taken 52
Chapter Thirteen: Wires And Roots...............57
Chapter Fourteen: Two Days 61
Chapter Fifteen: Towards the Hill..................66
Chapter Sixteen: The Quiet Surrender 70
Chapter Seventeen: The Bitter Branch 73
Chapter Eighteen: The World will Become Blackwood 77
Chapter Nineteen: The Five Keys 81
Chapter Twenty: The Silence Beyond 84
Chapter One: Waking in the Cold Hell..........89
Chapter Two: Rising From Ash and Earth 93
Chapter Three: The Detective.........................95
Chapter Four: Wings and Wires 97
Chapter Five: The First Wireborn 100
Chapter Six: The Fire....................................105
Chapter Seven: Perspective...........................108
Chapter Eight: The Frostline 111
Chapter Nine: Heaven's Hand 114
Chapter Ten: The Hand and the Harrow.....118

Chapter Eleven: The City of Frost 124
Chapter Twelve: The Visit Within 126
Chapter Thirteen: Tragedy in Frosthaven 129
Chapter Fourteen: Preparation 133
Chapter Fifteen: Inevitability 135
Chapter Sixteen: The World Notices 140
Epilogue: And a Bottle of Rum 143
Prologue: The Mutiny 149
Chapter One: The Boy 152
Chapter Two: Legends of the Dead Captain 156
Chapter Three: The Call of the Caves 161
Chapter Four: Punishment 165
Chapter Five: First Blood 169
Chapter Six: Ghosts of the Drowned 174
Chapter Seven: The Pact 179
Chapter Eight: The Drowning 183
Chapter Nine: The Dragging Deep 188
Chapter Ten: The Vessel 192
Chapter Eleven: Ink and Skin 196
Chapter Twelve: The Vessel Breaks 199
Chapter Thirteen: From the Shadows 203
Chapter Fourteen: The Last Fire 207
Chapter Fifteen: The Hollow Boy 211
Chapter Sixteen: The Groaning Choir 214
Chapter Seventeen: The Breaking of Chains 217
Chapter Eighteen: The First Mate 220
Special Thanks 223
Author's Note 224
A note on the Series 226
About the Author 227

Introduction

I would like to welcome you all to the Sour Worlds. What follows are stories that carry far more than they first appear. Each tale is a step deeper into places shaped by cruelty, loss, and ancient hatred. These worlds remember what has been done to them, and they do not forgive easily.

You will first walk the dark and ancient paths of Blackwood Forest, where the trees stand twisted with age and something vengeful waits just beyond sight. The forest is alive with memory, and what dwells within it has watched generations pass, feeding on fear and resentment. From there, you will be taken to the sprawling cities of Archcrest and Frosthaven, places of stone and ambition that stand proud against the coming dark. Within their walls, you will bear witness to The Harrow and feel the creeping frost of hell itself as it tightens its grip on the living. These cities are not safe havens, only stages for greater horrors to unfold.

Finally, we will journey back in time to the cursed waters of a forgotten age. From the depths, a dark pirate rises, pulled from death by forces long buried and best left undisturbed. With him comes rot, decay, and a spreading corruption that threatens to consume the world piece by piece. His return is not legend, but a warning.

This collection marks only the first step along a dark and dangerous path. What happens when three monsters rise and seek to claim the world for themselves? What happens when their paths

inevitably cross? These stories begin to answer
those questions, but the truth will only reveal
itself with time.

Prologue: The Vanishing

The forest was not quiet.
It breathed.

Ethan Price leaned against the cracked trunk of an old pine, wiping sweat from his brow with the back of his hand. The night was heavy around him, a damp weight pressing against his skin. The air reeked of rot, as though something had been left to fester beneath the soil for years.

He had been hiking alone for two days now, something his sister told him was reckless, stupid even, but Ethan was the kind of man who sought out quiet places where no one could follow. The ranger at the cabin warned him of entering Blackwood. Ethan did not heed the ominous warning. The forest here promised solitude. On the map it was marked as state land, but there were no signs, no trails, no campsites. Just green upon green, a smear of wilderness untouched by tourists.

Or so he thought.

Ethan had found strange things since setting camp that afternoon. Carvings on tree trunks, some crude, some careful: spirals, slashes, symbols he didn't recognize. On one trunk, a set of tally marks that stretched higher than he could reach, etched into the bark like someone had been keeping count.

He'd told himself it was the work of bored kids or hunters. He told himself a lot of things he didn't quite believe.

Now, as night pressed in and the forest seemed to close around him, those reassurances frayed thin.

The fire he built crackled weakly, not enough to push back the dark. The trees here grew so thick, so close together, the canopy strangled the moonlight before it could touch the ground. His little blaze looked like a candle swallowed by shadows.

And then a silence that felt like he was wearing earmuffs swallowed him. It was unnatural. The ambient noises of the night seemed to cut off abruptly.

A sound carried through the trunks. A shuffle. A creak. Not animal, not wind—something in between. Ethan froze with his spoon halfway to his mouth. The stew in the pot was still boiling, but he could no longer smell it over the sharp tang of moss and earth.

"Hello?" His voice cracked more than he intended and carried an unnatural distance in the muffled quiet.

The forest breathed back at him. The shuffle again, this time much closer.

Ethan's flashlight lay on the ground beside his tent. He reached for it slowly, fingers trembling, and flicked it on. The beam sliced through the dark, jittering as his hand shook.

At first he saw nothing. Only the endless, gnarled forest.

And then between two trees about thirty feet away he saw him.

A man.

At least, Ethan thought it was a man.

He stood perfectly still, too still, his body half-turned as though he'd just stepped out from behind one of the trees. His shape was human enough. Tall. Broad shouldered. Clothes hanging in tatters. From this distance Ethan could almost convince himself that the stranger was just another lost camper.

But the face.

The beam of the flashlight trembled over features that weren't right. What Ethan had thought was skin gleamed in wet ridges of bark. Moss spread down from the scalp like hair. And where eyes should have been, deep hollows gaped, shadows swallowing light.

Ethan stumbled back a step, the flashlight clattering from his hand. The beam spun wild across the trees, and in that spinning moment, the man was gone.

Ethan's breath came ragged. He backed toward the fire, hands shaking so badly he nearly tipped the pot into the flames. He told himself it was exhaustion. Hallucination. Shadows playing tricks.

Then bark cracked.

The sound was loud, sharp, like wood splintering under and enormous weight. Ethan swung around just in time to see movement, *out of the trunk.*

A giant hand pressed through the bark of a nearby tree, not breaking it but sliding out as if the wood were water. Fingers curled, made of dark wood and glistening moss. Then the rest of him followed, peeling from the trunk like a nightmare being shed from the forest itself.

The man, no, the giant thing stepped free. It was enormous. Bark shifted where skin should have been, creaking with each movement. The forest floor seemed to lean with him, roots twitching as he passed. He noticed all the sound was gone from the area as if someone flipped a switch.

Ethan bolted.

He ran blindly, crashing through brush with branches whipping at his face. His flashlight beam spun ahead, swinging with each desperate stride. He didn't care about the trail, didn't care about his pack, his tent, his fire. He only needed to get out.

But the forest did not let him.

The trees closed tighter, trunks crowding, roots tangling his steps. He tripped, fell hard, and scrambled up again, lungs burning. He thought he heard footsteps behind him, heavy but impossibly quick.

Then silence. Apart from him breathing heavily there were no other noises.

Ethan spun, chest heaving. Nothing. Only black trees and his own hammering heart.

He dared a single breath of relief.

And the bark behind him split.

Hands shot out, gripping his shoulders with the crushing strength of roots. Ethan screamed as the tree opened wider, swallowing him into darkness. The last thing he felt was the scrape of wood tightening against his skin, dragging him into the hollow.

The forest groaned as the bark closed again. The sounds of the forest came back. By morning, there was no sign of Ethan Price. Only a half-burned campfire, a dented flashlight, and a pot of stew gone cold.

The forest had breathed him in.

Part 1
Through The Trees

Chapter One: The Gathering

The road narrowed the deeper it went.

It had started as a respectable two-lane strip of cracked asphalt, weaving through farmland and the occasional rusted-out barn. But as the rented SUV rolled on, the lines faded, the shoulders vanished, and the trees pressed closer.

Branches arched overhead like ribs of some enormous creature, making a tunnel of shifting green. Every so often, the sunlight pierced through in sharp, surgical beams, and then it was gone again.

"GPS says fifteen more minutes," Jason announced from behind the wheel, tapping the dashboard as though the signal itself might hear him. His voice carried the calm confidence of someone who had been on more hikes than anyone else in the car combined. He wore mirrored sunglasses that reflected the tunnel of trees back at the others, hiding his eyes.

"Fifteen more minutes to what?" asked Amanda, slouched in the passenger seat. Her dark hair was pulled into a messy knot, and she had been nursing the same lukewarm coffee since they left town. "This road doesn't go anywhere. It's just... forest. You're sure this is even the right park?"

Jason smirked but didn't answer right away. He liked to let questions hang, make people lean toward him a little, wait for his response. "Trust me," he said finally. "I've been through here before. There's a trailhead. Little off the grid, but that's the point. No tourists, no screaming kids, no Wi-Fi."

"Perfect," muttered Kevin from the back seat, his face lit by the glow of his phone. "No Wi-Fi. How will I survive?"

"You won't," Amanda said dryly, and for the first time since morning, she almost smiled.

Beside Kevin, Lauren sat quietly, staring out the window. She hadn't spoken much since they left the diner two hours back. Her reflection in the glass looked pale, almost ghostlike against the blur of trees rushing past. She was the youngest of the group, invited mostly because she had no plans of her own and had said yes before she could think of a reason to say no.

The fifth seat, crammed in the way-back with backpacks and gear, belonged to Mark. He had earbuds in, head bobbing slightly, pretending not to listen to the bickering but catching every word anyway. When Jason announced, "fifteen more minutes," Mark muttered, "He's been saying that for half an hour."

Jason didn't hear him. Or pretended not to.

The SUV crested a hill, and suddenly the trees parted just enough to reveal a battered wooden sign at the roadside. The paint had long since faded, but the letters were still barely legible: **Blackwood State Forest.**

"See?" Jason said, triumphant, as though the sign had been placed there personally to prove him right.

"Blackwood," Amanda read aloud. "That's not ominous at all."

Kevin lowered his phone long enough to snap a picture. "Gonna add that to the group chat. Hashtag *murder trip*."

Lauren frowned at him. "Not funny."

Jason slowed the SUV as the road turned to gravel, the tires crunching over stone. The trees thickened here, pressing so close the mirrors nearly brushed them. Shadows slithered across the windshield, and the car seemed to sink into the green darkness.

They drove in silence for a while, the joking gone. The forest demanded quiet. Even Kevin put his phone down eventually.

Finally, the road ended in a crude parking lot carved out of dirt. Only one other car sat there: an old station wagon with mismatched panels, abandoned-looking.

Jason killed the engine. For a moment, the group just sat, listening to the sudden stillness. Without the hum of the motor, the forest seemed louder—the constant drone of insects, the restless rustle of unseen wings in the canopy.

"Well," Jason said, clapping his hands once. "Here we are. Blackwood. Home for the next three days."

"Three days?" Amanda turned on him. "You never said *three days*."

"Relax. It's not Everest. Just a couple of nights under the stars. We'll hike in, camp, loop back out. Easy."

Mark pulled an earbud free. "Easy, he says, while dragging us into the middle of nowhere."

Jason grinned. "Exactly."

They climbed out one by one, stretching limbs cramped from the drive. The air was cooler here, dense with the smell of pine and damp earth. The forest rose on all sides, swallowing the sky.

Lauren adjusted her pack straps nervously. "Doesn't it feel... I don't know. Quiet?"

"It's a forest," Jason said. "It's supposed to be quiet."

"No," Lauren insisted softly. "Not like this. I mean where are the birds?"

The others paused, listening. She was right. The buzzing of insects filled the air, but no bird calls broke the canopy. No chirps, no caws, no flutter of wings.

Amanda shivered despite herself. "I don't like it."

Jason forced a laugh, loud enough to shatter the tension. "You guys watch too many horror movies. It's just a forest. Trees, bugs, dirt. Nothing else."

But as he shouldered his pack and led the way toward the trailhead, a crooked wooden post barely visible among the undergrowth, even Jason kept glancing at the trees.

Because the forest was quiet. Too quiet.

And though none of them said it aloud, every one of them felt the same uneasy thought:

They were being watched.

The ranger's cabin was smaller than Amanda expected.

Jason had promised there would be a check-in point, somewhere official where they'd register before heading into the woods, but what stood before them looked more like a hunting shack than government property. The windows were clouded, the roof sagging under years of rot, and the porch boards were silvered with age. A crooked sign above the door read: **BLACKWOOD STATION.**

"Doesn't exactly scream 'welcome,'" Mark muttered as they approached.

Jason waved him off. "It's standard. Rangers don't care about paint jobs. They care about keeping idiots from setting the forest on fire." He adjusted the straps of his pack like he was proving a point, then strode up the steps and rapped his knuckles against the door. But the door was not made of wood like other ranger stations he had ever been to.

For a moment, nothing stirred. Then came the scrape of a chair leg inside, and the heavy door creaked open.

The man who filled the frame was tall but gaunt, his face leathered by years spent outdoors. His uniform had long since lost its crispness, the green shirt faded, the hat in his hand frayed at the brim. There was something odd about him that the group could not quite figure out. Something made him seem out of place. His eyes were dark, sharp, and they lingered on each of the hikers in turn. Each of the hikers felt the weight of the universe stare through their souls.

"You're late. I was hoping you wouldn't show up," the ranger said. His voice was low, almost gravelly.

Jason blinked. "Late?"

The man gestured at the sun already sagging westward. "Best time to hike in is morning. You lose the light faster than you think in these woods."

Jason laughed it off. "We've camped in worse. We'll be fine."

The ranger didn't return the smile. His gaze slid back to Amanda, to Kevin, to Lauren, as if weighing each of them in turn. "I would advise against going in but, I know you won't listen. Nobody ever does. Blackwood isn't like other forests," he said slowly as he motioned to the bulletin board to the left side of the door. "You stick to the marked path. Don't wander. And if you hear something in the night..." He trailed off, as though reconsidering his words.

Amanda tilted her head. "What do you mean 'if we hear something?'"

His dark eyes fixed on her. "Don't answer it."

The silence that followed was heavier than it should have been. Jason shifted, clearing his throat. "Noted. We'll be careful sir."

The ranger didn't move. His expression was unreadable, but his hands, Amanda noticed, clenched the doorframe as though he were resisting the urge to hold them back. Finally, with a faint shake of his head, he muttered, "Three days, you said?"

"Three days," Jason confirmed.

The ranger's jaw tightened. "Make it two."

Before any of them could reply, he closed the door. The click of the lock was louder than the closing itself.

They stood in silence for a long moment. Kevin was the first to break it. "Well. That wasn't creepy at all."

"Just an old guy trying to spook us," Jason said, forcing nonchalance. "He probably gives that speech to every group that comes through here."

"Yeah, but..." Amanda began, then stopped. She didn't know how to put it into words, the way the man's eyes had looked right *through* her. And seeing Ethan's picture on the bulletin board amongst the endless others sent chills down her spine. Instead, she tugged her jacket tighter and followed as Jason led the group toward the start of the trail.

The trailhead was little more than a break in the tree line, marked by a sun-bleached post with a faded arrow. Beyond it, the woods yawned wide and dark, swallowing the afternoon light whole.

The first steps in were hesitant. The dirt gave under their boots the smell of damp moss rising thick. Shafts of sunlight pierced the canopy in thin, slanted beams, but already the shadows seemed to dominate.

"Not so bad," Jason said, though his voice was softer than before.

They pushed deeper. The gravel crunch of the lot faded away behind them, swallowed by the forest. Insects buzzed unseen. The air cooled, thickening with an earthy scent that clung to the back of their throats.

Kevin lagged near the back, adjusting his straps. He was halfway through a quiet complaint about the weight of his pack when movement caught his eye.

Up ahead, beyond the tree line and slightly to the left, a hill rose above the canopy. He squinted. For a moment he thought it was just rocks, maybe a ridge catching the last of the sun. But then, movement again. Shapes.

Kevin slowed, letting the others drift further ahead while he focused. Yes. Definitely shapes. People.

There were at least four of them, maybe five. They stood in a line at the crest of the hill, motionless. All but one had binoculars raised to their faces, pointed directly at the hikers below. The last simply watched, hands folded in front of him.

Kevin blinked, unsettled. The figures were too far to make out details, but he could see enough to know they weren't rangers. These were locals.

He opened his mouth to say something *'Hey, does anyone else see that?'* but stopped himself.

What if it was nothing? Hunters. Birdwatchers. Weirdos with too much free time. If he pointed it out, Jason would mock him, Amanda would roll her eyes, and Mark would call him paranoid.

So, Kevin said nothing.

He pulled his gaze away, forcing his boots forward, and quickened his pace to catch up with the others. He told himself he imagined it.

That the shadows on the hill would be empty now if he looked again.

But as he rejoined the group and glanced back one last time, the figures hadn't moved.

They were still watching.

By the time the hikers reached the first mile marker, the sky was dimming fast. The forest felt heavier with each step, as though the trees themselves were bending closer, branches knitting overhead until the trail was a tunnel.

Jason kept the pace brisk, muttering that they'd make camp before sundown. Amanda trailed behind him, muttering complaints he ignored. Lauren stayed quiet, her eyes darting from tree to tree. Mark fiddled with his earbuds, pretending calm.

And Kevin, for the rest of the walk, never looked back again.

But he could feel the weight of unseen eyes.

Watching.

Always watching.

Always....

Chapter Three: Entering The Woods

The forest closed around them like a jaw.

By the time they had pushed past the third mile marker, the sun was already a faint smear of orange behind the canopy. The air grew darker with each step, as though the light itself was being swallowed. Every boot fall sank into damp earth, muffled, as if the forest wanted their presence to remain secret.

Jason called a halt at a shallow clearing beside the trail. It wasn't much but a patch of level ground where the trees bent back enough to show slivers of sky. A rotten log sat at the edge like a fallen guard, half-eaten by fungus.

"Here," Jason announced, dropping his pack. "Good enough for tonight."

Amanda planted her hands on her hips. "This is it? You promised scenic. This is... creepy."

"It's the woods, Amanda. It's supposed to be creepy." Jason smirked, but there was a tension in his voice now, the kind that suggested he wasn't as calm as he pretended.

Mark kicked at the ground, testing it. "Better than nothing. At least it's flat."

Lauren set her pack down carefully; her gaze fixed on the surrounding trees. She hadn't spoken much during the hike, but now she whispered, almost to herself, "They're too close."

"What?" Kevin asked.

"The trees. It feels like they're closer than when we started. Like the trail's getting thinner."

She caught herself and shook her head, embarrassed. "Never mind."

Kevin opened his mouth to say something maybe to mention what he'd seen on the hill earlier, but the words stuck in his throat. He swallowed them down, deciding once again to keep quiet.

Jason clapped his hands together. "All right. Tents up before dark. Chop chop."

The camp came together slowly. Jason's hands moved with practiced efficiency, hammering stakes, threading poles, snapping rain flies into place. Mark grumbled through the process, fumbling with knots until Jason barked at him to "just hold it steady." Amanda lit a small camp stove, swearing under her breath as she struggled with the ignition. Kevin halfheartedly helped where he could, more interested in sneaking glances at his phone, even though there was no service, he kept checking, as though bars might magically appear.

Lauren was the only one who kept drifting to the tree line, staring out as though expecting to see someone standing there. Each time Jason called her back, she returned reluctantly, but her eyes always strayed back to the dark between the trunks.

When at last the tents were standing and Amanda's pot of noodles was simmering, a fragile sense of comfort settled in. The forest pressed close, but the circle of camp felt safe — firelight painting their faces, the hiss of boiling water, the smell of propane masking the rot of moss.

They ate in relative silence, the tension of travel settled into fatigue. For a brief while, it almost felt like any other camping trip.

Almost.

The first sound came just as the stars began to show.

It was faint at first, a soft creak, like wood bending under strain. Jason froze mid-sentence, his spoon hovering over his bowl.

"What was that?" Amanda asked sharply.

"Tree settling," Jason said quickly. "Happens all the time."

But even he didn't sound convinced. There was a reason for all those posters on the bulletin board. Including their friend, Ethan Price.

The creak came again, longer this time. Then silence.

Kevin forced a laugh, thin and brittle. "Guys, it's a forest. Forests make noises. That's sort of what they do."

Mark grunted agreement and slurped another bite of noodles. But Amanda's eyes remained wide, and Lauren hugged her knees, staring into the dark.

The fire hissed, popping sparks.

Then came the whisper.

It slid through the trees like a draft, thin but distinct: a voice, low, stretched, impossible to place. None of them could make out words, but the cadence was unmistakable. Someone was speaking. Someone terribly close.

Amanda nearly dropped her bowl. "Tell me you heard that."

Jason's jaw clenched. He stood quickly, turning toward the sound. His flashlight beam cut across the trunks, shaking slightly in his hand. Nothing but trees stared back at them.

"It's just the wind," Jason said.

"That was *not* the wind," Amanda snapped.

But the whisper had already faded, leaving behind only the insect drone.

They argued in hushed tones for a while, each insisting on their version of reality. But eventually, fatigue won out. Tents zipped. Sleeping bags rustled. The fire dimmed to embers.

One by one, they settled in.

Kevin lay awake the longest.

He could not stop his mind from racing.

Who were those people on the ridge?

The others' breathing steadied around him, but sleep would not come. He stared at the thin nylon ceiling of his tent, every creak of the forest magnified tenfold. The image of the watchers on the hill wouldn't leave his mind. Nor would the ranger's warning: *don't answer it.*

A branch cracked somewhere deep in the woods. Kevin sat up, heart thudding, ears straining.

And then he heard it again.

The whisper.

Closer this time. Almost at the edge of camp.

He clamped a hand over his mouth, holding his breath.

The voice lingered for a long, aching moment before fading to silence.

Kevin lowered himself slowly back down, his pulse hammering in his throat. He didn't dare move again.

It was hours before sleep had finally taken him.

And when it did, he dreamed of bark splitting open, and a man-shaped shadow peeling out of a tree to stand beside his tent.

Watching.

The Knot.

The Tangles.

Always watching.

Chapter Four: The First Sign

The forest was a different place in the morning. As though they woke in a different reality altogether.

Mist clung low to the ground, curling around boots as the hikers packed up camp. Sunlight filtered weakly through the canopy, pale and reluctant, as though it resented the task. Everything was damp their tents, their clothes, even the air in their lungs.

Jason moved with brisk determination, rolling his gear with military precision. "We'll make better time today," he announced, glancing at the map pinned against a folded knee. "If we push, we should hit the ridge by late afternoon. Views are supposed to be incredible from up there."

Amanda muttered something about *views not being worth spiders in your shoes,* but she stuffed her sleeping bag into its sack all the same.

Mark stretched and let out a loud yawn. "As long as we don't get more creepy voices tonight, I'll call it a win."

Lauren, pale and quiet, paused at that. Her gaze had been drifting since dawn, lingering on the trees as though she expected them to blink. To move. At his words, she gave the faintest shake of her head.

Kevin kept silent. He hadn't told them about the whisper at his tent, nor about the watchers on the hill. Part of him half- assed believed that saying the words aloud would make them *too real.* And if no one else had heard, maybe... maybe it had been just his imagination.

Maybe.

Hopefully.

They set out single file, Jason leading, Amanda hot on his heels, then Lauren, Mark, and Kevin trailing. The trail was narrow, swallowed on either side by undergrowth. Spiderwebs caught the light, silver filaments swaying in the breeze.

The first mile passed in relative quiet, their conversation sparse. But near the second marker, Lauren stopped abruptly.

"Look," she whispered.

At first none of them saw it. Then Jason followed her gaze and swore under his breath.

The tree to their right was carved. Not initials or hearts like a lover's graffiti. These marks were deliberate, deep gouges that formed long vertical lines up the trunk. Dozens of them, reaching higher than any of them could.

"More tally marks," Jason muttered. "Like the ones I saw yesterday."

"Counting what?" Amanda asked, voice low.

Jason shrugged, but it was a stiff, uneasy motion. "Hunters. Probably tracking kills."

"Those aren't from a knife," Mark said flatly. "Look closer."

They leaned in. He was right. The grooves weren't clean — they were ragged, like something with claws had raked them. The wood puckered around the edges, scarred from repeated strikes.

Amanda stepped back quickly. "Nope. Done. Out. We're leaving."

Jason frowned. "We just got here."

"This place is wrong, Jason! A ranger practically begged us not to go in, we're hearing voices, and now this..."

She stopped mid-sentence.

Because the forest had gone silent.

The insects. The distant rustle of wings. The drip of water from the canopy. All gone.

The sudden quiet pressed against their ears like heavy cloth. Kevin clapped a hand to his head instinctively, as though trying to remove invisible earmuffs.

"Do you hear that?" Lauren whispered. Her voice carried unnaturally far, echoing faintly through the trunks.

"Yes," Amanda hissed. "It's, God, it's too quiet."

Jason tried to laugh, but it faltered. "Just a lull. Animals stop sometimes."

"No," Lauren said firmly, her voice quivering despite her certainty. "This isn't animals. It's *something else.*"

The air grew heavier. Oppressive. An angry silence. Their own breathing sounded too loud, ragged against the hush.

Then, just at the edge of the trail, came the whisper.

Longer now. Clearer. Like a voice underwater, stretched and blurred. But there were words hidden inside it, fragments clawing their way through the silence.

"...come... come back..."

Amanda clutched Jason's arm. "What did it say?"

"Nothing." Jason's jaw was set hard. "It didn't say anything. Just... wind."

Kevin swallowed hard. The sound carried, twisting through the trunks. He wanted to scream at Jason, *stop lying, we all heard it,* but the words tangled in his throat.

The whisper swelled again, lower this time. The syllables fractured but insistent:

"...stay... forever..."

Lauren covered her ears, shaking her head. "Make it stop. Make it stop."

And then, just as suddenly as it began, it ended.

The forest exhaled. Insects chirped. Leaves rustled. A crow cawed above, sharp, and abrupt, and they all jumped at the sound.

The noise returned all at once, overwhelming after the vacuum of silence.

The hikers stood frozen, staring at one another.

Jason was the first to move. He slung his pack higher and forced a steady voice. "We keep moving. Don't stop. Just keep moving."

No one argued.

Two miles later, they found the handprint.

It was smeared across the bark of a crooked birch just off the trail. Dark, dried, and unmistakably human. The fingers dragged downward, as though the owner had clawed for purchase.

Amanda gagged. "Is that..."

"Yes," Jason cut in quickly. "Paint. Just paint."

Kevin crouched, studying it. The edges of the print were cracked and the grooves filled with moss. Old, but not old enough. He touched the bark near it still faintly tacky.

"Definitely not paint," Kevin whispered.

Jason grabbed his shoulder and hauled him upright. "I said it's paint." His voice was sharp, commanding. But his eyes... his eyes betrayed something else. He knew.

They all knew.

For the rest of the day all conversation was kept at a minimum. Not intentionally but their minds were heavy with thought. They walked faster, boots pounding the dirt, each glance over the shoulder sharper than the last.

But every now and then, when the forest dipped into silence again, Kevin caught Amanda's lips moving soundlessly.

She was counting.

He didn't need to ask what.

That night, when they made camp again, no one mentioned the whisper. No one mentioned the handprint.

But as Kevin lay awake, staring at the ceiling of his tent, he couldn't help thinking of the tally marks.

And the possibility that each mark wasn't for a deer or a bear.

Each was for a person.

And the count was still rising.

Chapter Five: Lauren's Dream

Lauren had struggled to find sleep that night, and when sleep finally took her in its embrace, it was not comforting. Not at all.

She could hear the others in their tents shifting positions to find a comfortable spot on the hard ground. When she finally closed her eyes she was in an empty space, floating in the darkness. In the distance she could make out a shape in the voided space. It appeared to be moving toward her, slowly, each step taking an eternity.

Closer and closer it got but she was frozen in place unable to move out of fear of what may happen. Closer. And closer still. It resembled the shape of a human, but it was tall.

As the figure stepped toward her she could see more and more details. Its face lacked a mouth, but the eyes, the eyes were gaping hollows that had tendrils of void darkness emanating from them like smoke from a fire.

The giant figure moved closer still. Once it got within arm's reach it stopped. The figure seemed to be studying her, but it did not say a word.

Lauren broke the silence within her dream.

"What are you?" she asked the giant figure softly.

The giant thing tilted its head slightly as if curious. Silence filled the air. The creature lifted its arm and stretched it towards her slowly as if it were trying to grab something that was extremely delicate.

The beast extended one finger from its giant hand and brushed a strand of hair from her face and then it spoke to her.

"Lauren....... I know why you are here my child. You seek a lost friend. You are not here for an adventure." The great beast spoke to her as though he was a loving parent consoling their distraught child. "You ask what I am..... I am the forest. I am every tree you see. Every leaf. Every root cut through the dirt. I am The Knot that ties the forests together."

"What do you want from us?" Lauren whispered softly.

The great beast seemed to think on this for a moment. Digging up an answer.

"You all have no choice. You have crossed the barrier into my domain. The ranger warned you all of entering Blackwood. Yet you did not heed the warning. My Tangles have told of your presence." The Knot replied.

"We had to know if he was still alive. He's our friend. We were worried. The last known location from him before going dark was right outside these woods before the signal drops off." Lauren spat out at him with a hint of hysterics in her voice.

The Knot did not respond right away. In his mind he was judging the intentions of the group. He felt they were what he needed, but he needed to see how they would react when backed into a corner.

In silence Lauren's thoughts raced. She did not know what this creature was. But she knew they were trapped now for sure.

"You all will be tested in this forest." The beast stated as he turned away and faded into the voided space of her dream.

Lauren called out to the beast, but he was already gone. She was left alone in the empty space of her dream. She didn't know how long she was alone, but she could now hear a voice. At first it was low, almost too low to hear. It grew in volume gradually, whispers she couldn't make out words that weren't fully formed.

In a flash a figure appeared before her. It was Ethan Price. He was right in front of her, nose to nose.

"Give in to the forest Lauren!" Ethan shouted.

He kept repeating the words over and over each time louder than the last. Lauren covered her ears, but it did not black out the screaming.

The screaming stopped suddenly, and she could see Ethan had closed his eyes. Silence took over. Ethan did not move. Lauren was frozen, unable to speak. It was as though the words were lost to her as well as her voice.

In an instant Ethan disappeared leaving Lauren alone in the empty space again. She reached out to see if she could feel anything. Nothing. She retreated her hand and a figure appeared suddenly and grabbed her.

"Give in to the forest!" shouted the thing.

It looked like Ethan, but he was constructed of roots and moss and twigs. It was wrong.

In the tent Lauren jumped from her sleeping bag with horror in her eyes. Should she tell the others? No, they would just say she is crazy.

She thought of the city she called home. Frosthaven. She longed to be in her bed at home. But it was her that put the idea of going to these haunted woods in Jason's mind. She had hoped to find their friend. They all knew Ethan but not as well as Lauren knew him. They had grown up together in Archcrest. Her mom loved to see him come by and visit. Lauren loved to see him.

A part of her was glad he went by himself on this trip. Another part was afraid of what the great beast said and what the vision of Ethan had told her. 'Give in to the forest.'

What does that mean?

Lauren thought about the dream while they all rolled up their gear to start the new day.

Chapter Six: The Tangles

By the third day, the forest felt endless. They had followed the narrow trail until Jason swore they should have reached the ridge. Every path looking the same. Roots clawed across the dirt, trunks pressed close, branches laced overhead until the light itself seemed caught in the trees just out of sight.

Amanda stopped in the middle of the trail and dropped her pack. "We're lost."

Jason turned, jaw tight. "We are not lost. The map..."

"The map doesn't matter," she snapped. Her face was pale with exhaustion, sweat plastering hair against her forehead. "We've been circling the same damned trail markers for hours. Just admit it Jason."

Jason glanced at the carved post ahead weather-beaten, tilted then back at the one they had passed not but twenty minutes ago. Identical. For the first time, he did not argue.

Kevin sank onto a rock, breathing heavily. His phone was dead now, and part of him was glad. At least it couldn't remind him how cut off they were. He stared at the dirt between his boots, and for a moment he thought he saw it shift, as if something beneath was breathing. He blinked, and it was still again.

Lauren stood rigid, staring into the trees. "Someone's there."

All eyes turned to her.

She didn't blink, didn't move. Her hand trembled as she raised it, pointing toward the shadowed undergrowth to the right.

At first, they saw nothing. Just trees, vines, and the tangle of brush.

Then Kevin's stomach dropped.

It was a figure.

Shaped like a man, maybe six feet tall, shoulders hunched, body woven from sticks and vines twisted tightly together. Moss dangled like flesh, and branches knotted into the rough suggestion of arms and legs. Its face, if it could be called that, was an approximation: hollows for eyes, a knot of twigs for a mouth.

It stood utterly still.

Jason's voice cracked as he whispered, "What the hell is that?"

As if in answer, the thing tilted its head. Not much, just a fraction. Enough to show it had heard.

Lauren whimpered.

Jason grabbed his flashlight, but before he could aim it, the forest changed.

The bugs stopped. The rustle of leaves froze. The sound drained away so suddenly it was like someone had pulled heavy earmuffs over their ears. Their own breathing roared inside their skulls. Amanda's sharp inhale echoed unnaturally, carrying farther than it should have.

Silence.

Kevin whispered, terrified, "It's close."

And though none of them said the name, they all knew what he meant.

The Knot.

The figure, the *Tangle*, moved.

Not toward them. Not away. It simply shifted, like a tree bending against a breeze that wasn't there. The creak of vines carried through the deadened air.

Then, from deeper within the woods came another sound: a matching creak.

And another.

And another.

Every one sounding closer than the last.

Shapes emerged between the trunks. One. Two. Five. More. All made of sticks, vines, bark, and moss, each twisted into rough human forms. Some were small like children, some tall, one with a crooked limb dragging behind like that of someone nursing a broken limb.

The hikers stood paralyzed as dozens of eyeless hollows turned their way in unison.

Amanda's voice trembled. "They're... people."

"No," Jason hissed. "They're *things.*"

But Kevin understood. The proportions were not random. The shapes were not arbitrary. Each shape was a grotesque echo of someone who had once lived. Shoulders too sloped, arms too long, jaws too wide. But behind the distortions, Kevin could *see* the resemblance. One even had a tattered scrap of fabric clinging to its vine-shoulder, the remains of a red flannel shirt.

They had been hikers once. Campers. People like them.

Lauren's hand covered her mouth, stifling a sob.

The silence deepened. It was suffocating. And then, threading through it, came the whisper.

This time it was not the distant, stretched voice from before. This was hundreds of voices overlapping, speaking in broken fragments.

"...stay..."

"...watching..."

"...come closer..."

"...roots... bind..."

The words bled together, carried too far in the muffled air. Each syllable was theirs and not theirs, pulled from mouths that were no longer human.

Amanda backed up until she nearly collided with Jason. "They're talking."

Jason forced a steady tone, though his face had gone pale. "No. They're mimicking. Just noise. Ignore it."

But the whispers grew louder, fractured voices rising in a hive's chorus.

"...hungry... stay... one of us... always..."

Lauren broke first. She turned and bolted back the way they had come, crashing down the trail.

"Lauren!" Jason shouted. He sprinted after her, the others stumbling to follow.

Behind them, the Tangles did not chase.

They simply turned their vine-heads as one. The empty eyes tracking, still whispering.

Watching.

Always watching.

They did not stop running until their lungs gave out. By then, the noises of the forest had returned. Crickets, rustles, the drip of water, all of it overwhelming in its suddenness.

Lauren collapsed against a tree, gasping. "They're following us. I swear they're following us."

"They didn't move," Jason said, bending double, hands on his knees. Sweat ran down his face. "They were just... standing there."

"That's worse!" Amanda snapped. "That's so much worse!"

Kevin looked back down the trail. Nothing but shadows. But he could not shake the feeling that dozens of hollow eyes were still turned their way.

He swallowed hard. "What if... what if those things aren't just... things? What if they're... what's left?"

The others stared at him.

"You mean people," Amanda whispered.

Kevin nodded. "People who got lost here before. People taken by the forest."

Jason straightened, shaking his head hard. "No. No, we're not doing this. They're not people. They're... I don't know. Some kind of local scarecrow trick. Moss puppets. Whatever. But not people."

But his voice cracked on the last word, and no one believed him.

That night, camp was worse than the last.

Every creak of branches sounded like vines shifting. Every whisper of wind felt like a voice at their ear. And when the silence fell again, brief but heavy, they clung to one another, eyes wide in the dark.

No one slept deeply.

Because they all knew the truth now.

They weren't alone in the forest.

The forest had an army.

And it was made of everyone who had come before them.

By the time dusk settled, the hikers had stopped pretending this was an adventure.

Chapter Seven: Night of the Tangles

The forest had stripped the idea away from them, mile by mile, until only survival remained. Jason no longer spoke of ridges or scenic views. Amanda had stopped arguing and instead marched in grim silence. Lauren trailed behind with glassy eyes, pale as if she were walking in a fever. Even Mark, who had met every complaint with sarcasm before, now muttered only curses under his breath.

Kevin carried the weight of words unsaid. The watchers on the hill. The whispers outside his tent. The truth about the handprint. But most of all, he carried the certainty that what they had seen, those *Tangles*, weren't finished with them.

The forest agreed.

Every time their voices rose above a murmur, the woods answered with silence. Not a gradual lull, but an abrupt, suffocating hush the "earmuff" stillness that warned of the Knot's nearness. In those moments, the group froze, afraid even to breathe. And when sound returned, it was always too much, overwhelming, as if the forest were trying to prove it had never stopped at all.

By the time they made camp, the air itself felt taut, stretched to the point of breaking.

They chose a clearing narrower than the others, their tents pitched almost touching. Amanda argued that closer was safer, and for once, no one disagreed. The fire was small, barely more than a glow between them, but they sat huddled around it as though it could keep back the things outside.

Dinner was silent. Even Jason didn't try to rally them. He chewed mechanically, eyes darting to the tree line.

Mark broke the quiet first. "We should leave."

Jason looked up sharply. "We can't."

"Why not?"

"Because we don't know where we are." Jason slapped the map against his thigh. "It doesn't make sense. None of this does. But if we just keep moving..."

"Moving where?" Amanda snapped. "Every direction looks the same. We're not getting out."

The fire popped, scattering sparks.

Lauren whispered, "They'll let us out when they're finished with us."

Everyone stared at her.

She sat cross-legged, staring into the fire. Her expression was blank, her voice toneless, like she was speaking from a dream. "That's what the voices said last night. That's what they always say."

Jason reached for her shoulder. "Lauren, don't—"

The forest fell silent.

All sound snuffed out at once, insects, wind, the distant call of night birds, all of them gone.

The group froze.

Amanda's breath hitched too loudly, echoing across the clearing.

Mark's spoon slipped from his hand and clattered against the pot. The metallic ring carried and carried until it felt like the whole forest was listening.

Kevin's skin crawled. He knew what was coming.

From the dark came the whisper.

"...closer... closer..."

"...watching... through you..."

The voices carried, overlapping, hundreds at once. The words seemed to leak from every trunk, every branch, until the clearing itself was speaking.

And then, between the trees, Kevin saw them.

The Tangles.

One stood at the edge of the clearing, motionless, vines glistening in the firelight. Another behind it, hunched and crooked. And another. And another.

Dozens.

They surrounded the camp in a wide ring, all facing inward, heads tilted at unnatural angles.

Lauren rose to her feet slowly, her eyes wide but glassy, as if she were listening to something the others couldn't hear. "They're not supposed to move in daylight," she murmured.

Jason grabbed her arm and pulled her back toward the fire. "Stay with us."

The nearest Tangle creaked, its vine-limbs groaning as it shifted one step closer.

The whispering surged.

"...join... join us..."

"...roots... tangled... never gone..."

Mark stumbled back, nearly tripping over his tent. "Oh my God. They're alive. They're *alive.*"

Jason yanked his knife from its sheath. "Stay behind me."

But the blade looked pitiful compared to what stood before them, an army of corpses reimagined in wood and moss, hollow and endless.

Amanda screamed.

Not because of the Tangles in front of them.

But because when she turned, there was one behind her tent, half inside the clearing already. Its arms bent wrong, twisted vines reaching forward like fingers.

The silence thickened.

The Tangles all stepped forward at once.

Not fast. Not lunging. But slow, deliberate, in perfect unison, like marionettes drawn by the same hand. Each creak of their vines carried like thunder in the muffled air.

Closer.

Closer.

Kevin couldn't breathe. He thought of the watchers on the hill, of the tally marks carved high in the trees, of the handprint dragging down bark. He understood now, the Knot didn't just kill. It collected. It rewove what it had taken into new shapes, new servants. Extensions of itself.

The Tangles were its eyes. Its ears.

And soon, they would be in its hands.

"Run," Kevin whispered.

The word carried unnaturally far in the silence, echoing through the ring of Tangles like an invitation.

For a heartbeat, no one moved.

Then Jason slashed his knife at the air, shouting, "Run!"

They bolted into the trees, scattering into the dark, the fire left behind to die.

Behind them, the Tangles did not chase.

They simply turned, vines creaking, watching as the hikers fled deeper into the forest.

And somewhere, hidden in silence, the Knot smiled through them all.

Chapter Eight: The Hunt in Silence

They ran until the firelight was gone.

The forest swallowed them in an instant, shadows clawing across their path, branches lashing at their faces. They didn't stop to think, didn't stop to plan. They just ran, boots thudding in frantic rhythm against the dirt.

Jason led, slashing at vines with his knife, Amanda close on his heels. Mark stumbled behind, cursing between ragged breaths. Kevin and Lauren trailed last, Lauren clutching Kevin's arm so tightly her nails dug through his sleeve.

Only when their legs burned and their lungs threatened to collapse did Jason pull them into a hollow between two leaning trunks. "Quiet," he hissed, forcing the word out between gasps. "Just quiet."

They pressed against the trees, sucking air, straining to hear past the pounding of their hearts.

For a moment, all was still.

Then came the creak.

Not from one place. From everywhere.

Vines groaning. Sticks bending. The slow, patient sound of the Tangles moving.

Amanda covered her mouth, muffling a sob.

Kevin peered back through the darkness. At first he saw nothing. Then, faintly, the outline of a Tangle shifting between trees. Another behind it. Another to the left.

They weren't running.

They were closing in, step by step, moving in the same terrible unison. Herding.

Jason swore under his breath. "We keep moving. Stay low. Stay together."

They crept through the undergrowth, trying to silence each step. But the forest betrayed them. Every snapped twig, every rustle in the brush, carried through the air like a gunshot.

And then, without warning, silence fell.

The forest sounds vanished, smothered all at once.

The world pressed in, heavy and suffocating. Their ears rang with the sudden absence. Voices carried too far, too sharp. The muffled hush of the Knot's nearness.

Jason froze mid-step. Amanda clutched his arm.

From the dark, the whispers began.

"...you cannot run..."

"...you are roots now..."

"...always... with me..."

The words echoed from trunk to trunk, overlapping, fractured. Some were deep and hollow, others high and keening, but they all spoke in the same cadence.

Kevin's blood ran cold. He recognized one of the voices.

It was Ethan Price's. The missing camper whose name had been scribbled in old newspaper clippings Jason showed them when convincing them to come here. He had been gone for almost two years, yet his voice bled through the Tangles as though he had whispered only yesterday.

Kevin stumbled back, shaking his head. "It's them. It's *all of them*. They're still here."

Mark's face twisted in panic. "Shut up, just shut up!"

But Kevin couldn't. He could feel it now. The whispers weren't just voices—they were *paths.* Threads running through the trees, carrying not just sound but memory, essence. Through them, the Knot could stretch himself beyond the bark, beyond the forest.

And into them.

The group pressed on, weaving blindly through the maze of trunks, trying to keep to the trail but losing it again and again. Each time they thought they'd gained ground, the silence fell, and the Tangles were there, closer, waiting.

They didn't lunge. They didn't chase.

They simply *were.*

Watching. Closing in.

Lauren tripped, falling to her knees. Kevin hauled her up, whispering frantically, "Don't stop. Please, don't stop."

But when she stood, she didn't look at him. Her eyes were wide, glazed, her lips moving silently.

Jason snapped his fingers in front of her face. "Lauren, hey. Focus."

She blinked, shuddered, and then broke into a sob. "They're inside me. I hear them. All of them. They're not dead. They're tangled."

Her words carried too loudly in the muffled air. The Tangles responded with a low groan of vines, a hundred bodies shifting at once.

Jason pulled her forward. "We move. Now."

And so they stumbled deeper into the dark.

They did not see the Knot that night.

But they felt him.

Every silence was his. Every whisper was his.
And every step carried them further into his
design.

Perspective: The Knot

The forest breathed with him.

Through the trees he stretched, roots beneath the soil, branches above the sky. His body was not bark and moss, not entirely, though he wore those things as one might wear clothes. His body was *all that had been tangled into him.*

The girl had heard correctly.

They were not dead, the ones he had taken. They were never dead. They had been broken, unwoven, and rewoven into him. Their voices were his voices now. Their eyes, his eyes. Their memories, his doors.

The Tangles stood where he placed them, extensions of his mind, puppets with no strings. Through them he watched. Through them he listened. Through them he whispered back into the ears of the living, baiting them, drawing them deeper.

Every step the hikers took belonged to him already.

But he was not satisfied.

The forest was vast, yes. But the world beyond it was vaster still. And he missed his forests in the world. Ever since the barrier appeared and confined him to this patch of woods. He has been trapped here for far too long with only small glimpses into the world

And he hungered for it.

He had learned the way: through the voices of the tangled, he could pass along their memories, their homes, their loved ones. Already, he could see the edges of doorways far beyond this forest, carried on the echoes of lives he had swallowed.

Unable to step through, but he could see beyond Blackwood.

Soon, he would not be bound to Blackwood.

Soon, every tree, every wooden door, every beam in every house would be his gate.

And when that day came, there would be no escaping him.

He would collect *everyone*.

Everywhere.

The forest shuddered with his hunger.

And the Knot smiled through his tangles.

Chapter Nine: The Knot's Journey

Before there were men, there were trees. The first roots dug into the soil of Blackwood when the land was still raw, when rivers cut their courses in wild violence and hills shifted like the backs of sleeping beasts. Rain fell unbroken by roofs, lightning split the sky without witnesses.

And in that stillness, something opened its eyes.

It was not born. It was not created. It was simply awake.

The Knot.

He rose as the first seed cracked open and reached toward the sun. He felt the roots curl downward into the dark, fingers of hunger digging into the soil. He felt the sap climb the veins of bark, the breath of leaves unfolding in the dawn. He ventured around the world and sprouted great forests all over the barren world.

He tended to them. Watched them. Fed them.

Not as a gardener tends, but as a parent does: fiercely, jealously, without question.

He was the space between roots, the hush between branches. He was the silence that fell when the forest listened to itself.

And he was content.

The seasons cycled. Green to gold to black to green again. He whispered through the canopy, stirring leaves into song. He pressed saplings from seed to sprout, wound roots into tangled strength, guided vines to their climb.

When fire came, born of lightning, he smothered it with rain. When rot festered, he consumed it, weaving new life from the decay.

The forest was whole. Perfect.

Until they came.

The first men arrived long before Blackwood had a name. Hunters and wanderers, clad in skins, carrying fire where their hands could not reach. They cut paths through undergrowth, broke branches, dug pits. They burned.

The Knot watched.

At first, he thought they were animals clumsy, blind, driven by the same needs as the deer and the fox. But animals took what they needed and no more. These... things... took without end. They cut trees not for shelter, not for warmth, but for sport. For noise. For nothing.

The forest screamed as trunks fell, their voices silenced forever. Roots were torn from the earth, exposed to the pitiless sky. The Knot felt each wound as his own.

He whispered warnings, the groan of bending boughs, the crash of branches in their path, storms that rose sudden and fierce. Still they came.

Still they cut.

And so, the Knot began to collect.

The first to vanish was a hunter who had wandered too far, his fire smoldering where it fell. The Knot slipped through bark and root, and when the man turned, the forest swallowed him whole. His voice became the Knot's voice. His memory became the Knot's path.

Others followed. One by one, those who strayed too deep became tangled in his grasp.

Their bodies unwoven, their souls rewoven, their shapes rebuilt in vines, sticks, and moss. They became his extensions. His guardians. His warning to the others.

But the others did not listen.

Men did what men always did. They came in greater numbers. They cut more trees.

And then they built.

The cabin was small, hardly more than four walls and a roof. But its presence was an insult. A scar raised against centuries of balance.

The Knot felt it the moment it was planted. Posts hammered into the soil like spears. Logs stacked where trunks had fallen. Smoke twisting from a chimney that bled the air.

But it was not the wood that angered him most.

It was the defiance.

The cabin did not rot. It did not weaken. Its walls were lined, shielded, bound with something that broke his passage. Metal. The forest could not move through it. He could not move through it.

Inside, men huddled safe, their fires burning, their voices mocking the silence.

The Knot's rage spread through roots and branches. His hunger deepened.

It was then he swore:

He would rid the forest of the infestation.

He would rid the world of it.

The years passed. Rangers came and went. Trails carved deeper. Roads paved to carry more of them into his heart. Each year, more boots, more fire.

But with each, he collected more.

Every hiker who wandered too far, every camper who strayed, every child who followed whispers into the dark, all of them tangled into him, woven into his hive of silence.

The Knot grew stronger.

Through the voices of his victims, he learned. He saw their towns, their homes, their families. He felt the wood in their houses, their doors, their tables, all the places he might one day pass through.

But he was still bound to Blackwood.

He was only waiting for the right things to line up.

There was something else he needed.

The Keys.

The hikers did not know this, not yet. They stumbled in the dark, unaware they were walking inside the oldest promise the forest had ever made.

But the Knot knew them.

He knew their faces, their fears, their voices.

And soon, he would know their homes.

He would not stop at Blackwood.

He would not stop at all.

The forest was only the beginning.

Chapter Ten: Children of the Knot

The Knot had no need for memory, yet he carried centuries of them. Each voice tangled into him left behind a story. Each story bled into his roots, into his whispers. They belonged to him now.

And though time blurred, some moments remained sharp, as though he wanted the forest to remember.

The Woodcutter

He was the first to learn.

An old man with an axe, back bent from years of labor. He believed the forest owed him its limbs, that every tree was his to cut. He took without pause, without reverence, stacking wood until it reached the height of his house.

The Knot watched as he felled a birch that had grown for a hundred years. Its scream echoed in silence only the Knot could hear.

That night, when the man stumbled home, the forest followed him. He locked his wooden door, certain he was safe. But a door made of wood is no door at all to the Knot.

The man's screams carried far, muffled by silence, until the forest swallowed him whole. His axe rusted where it fell.

The trees grew taller over it.

The Lovers

Two young hikers, tangled together in secret. They wandered off trail, away from lantern light, chasing a place where no one could see them.

But someone always sees.

The Knot slipped between trunks, closer and closer, until silence fell. The boy heard it first, pulling away from her laughter, glancing at the woods that now seemed too still. He whispered her name, and the forest whispered it back.

She ran. He followed. Their hands reached for each other but never touched again.

By dawn, both were tangled. Their shapes still stand side by side, vines woven between them like fingers interlaced.

The Ranger

The first ranger who built the cabin thought himself to be a guardian of the woods. He patrolled with his rifle in hand, carving paths, hammering posts, leaving markers to guide the lost.

But he was not the guardian.

He felt the Knot watching him in the hush between the calls of the owls. He dreamed of branches curling through the cracks of his cabin, reaching for him as he slept.

He lasted a year.

When he vanished, they said he left his post, abandoned his duty. But the Knot knew better. The forest had taken him. Only the cabin remained, a hollow shell that would pass from ranger to ranger, each believing it was theirs.

But the Knot would never forget the first.

His Tangle still walked near the cabin at night, a hollow figure of vines and bark, eyes turned toward the place he once called home. This was when the barrier appeared, further angering The Knot.

The Boy

He was the youngest.

His family had come for a weekend. A father with tired hands, a mother with gentle eyes, and their child — no older than eight. They laughed as they unpacked their car, carrying gear too new, too bright. The forest watched.

That night, the Knot came.

The boy awoke to silence. He heard whispers through the canvas of the tent, voices like his parents' but wrong, stretched too far, calling his name.

When he peered outside, his father was standing by the fire. Too still. His mother beside him, her face hidden in shadow.

"Come here," they whispered.

He stayed inside. Curled into his sleeping bag, trembling, he waited for the whispers to fade.

By morning, they were gone. Their shoes were still by the fire. Their bowls were half full. But they were gone.

For two days, the boy survived alone. He ate dry cereal from a bag, drank rainwater from his hands, and cried himself into exhaustion.

On the third night, he wandered.

The silence fell again, heavy and smothering. He felt it like a blanket pulled too tight.

When the whispers came, they were not his parents' this time. They were his own.

"Come here," the forest said in his voice.

He ran. But children do not outrun roots.

The Knot opened the bark for him, vines curling around his small limbs, pulling him into the dark.

By dawn, he was gone.

Now, when hikers wander too far, they sometimes see a small figure among the Tangles. Twigs for fingers. Moss for hair. The faint outline of a child's face in the hollows.

He does not speak, except to whisper in voices that are not his.

But he watches.

Always watching.

The Knot remembered them all.

Each voice another root. Each root another voice.

And he was still hungry.

Chapter Eleven: The Knot's Vision

The Knot felt them before he saw them.

Five new voices, warm and loud, thrumming with the pulse of blood and thought. Their boots pressed into the soil of Blackwood as if they belonged here, as if their right to walk was equal to his right to exist. He felt each step like a thorn, each laugh like a wound.

They were not the first, but they were different.

Most who wandered his forest were small in scope. A family. A farmer. A lover. They belonged to a single hearth, a single road, a single place. Their voices gave him paths only as wide as their roots. Through them he learned about their homes, their cabins, their narrow worlds.

But these five...

These five belonged to many places.

He tasted it in their whispers.

The tall one with the knife, Jason, had walked other trails, far from Blackwood. His voice carried echoes of mountain ranges, desert canyons, and peaks where no trees grew. He thought himself untouchable because he had touched so much land. Through him, the Knot could spread into stone, into desert, into barren ranges where roots should never cling.

The sharp-tongued woman, Amanda, carried cities in her blood. He heard the echo of subway tunnels, the rattling of trains, the wood in beams hidden beneath concrete and steel. She thought of herself as a creature of glass and iron, but wood always remained. Through her, the Knot could seep into cities, where millions huddled.

The quiet girl, Lauren, carried generations of voices. Her ancestors had called other forests home, far to the north, where snow buried trunks to their crowns. He heard the tundra in her breath, the whisper of birches in lands she had never walked but still belonged to her. Through her, he could stretch into the frozen world, where roots slumbered beneath ice.

The boy with the phone, Kevin, was tethered to everywhere. His voice was cluttered with the noise of a thousand connections, places spoken to but never touched. The Knot did not yet understand the wires and signals that bound him, but he recognized their power. Through him, he would not only spread across soil, but across thought.

And the bitter one, Mark, carried only bitterness. He belonged to no place, no path, no hearth. But even rootless branches serve their purpose. Through him, the Knot would reach the forsaken edges, the forgotten places, where silence already ruled.

The Knot marveled.

Never before had such a group come together. Never before had so many paths crossed in a single place.

To take them would be to open doors.

They are the keys to a bigger world.

Not just in Blackwood. Not just in the cabins, the camps, the logging roads.

Everywhere.

He saw it now: through Jason's mountains, Amanda's cities, Lauren's frozen woods,

Kevin's wires, Mark's forgotten roads. They were carriers. Seeds.

Through them, he could root himself across the world.

Through them, he could become civilization's end.

The Tangles stirred, reflecting his hunger. They shifted in the dark, whispering fragments of the new voices, mimicking words that had barely left their lips. They watched, always watching, until the hikers began to feel eyes on them even in dreams.

The Knot pressed closer.

Every silence was his hand. Every whisper was his breath.

They thought themselves hunters, explorers, travelers. They thought they were moving of their own will.

But the Knot had already bound them.

They would not escape.

And when they were tangled, their roots would split wide and far, carrying him through every door, every tree, every wooden bone of their false civilization.

The infestation called *man* had spread too long.

Now the forest would answer.

Now the Knot would grow.

Forever.

Chapter Twelve: The First Taken

The fire was low.

They huddled close to it as though the flames could keep away the silence. Shadows danced across pale faces, each of them drawn tight with fatigue and unspoken fear.

It was Kevin who broke first.

"I saw them."

The others turned. His voice had been soft, almost lost to the hiss of the fire, but it carried too far in the muffled air.

Jason frowned. "Saw what?"

"The locals. When we first came in. Up on the hill." Kevin's throat was dry, his hands trembling as he spoke. "They were standing there, watching us. With binoculars."

Amanda blinked. "Binoculars?"

"Yes." Kevin's voice rose, sharp with the weight of carrying the secret for too long. "A whole group of them. Just watching. Like they were waiting for us. And I didn't say anything because I didn't want to freak you out, but..."

"Jesus Christ, Kevin." Jason's jaw tightened. "You've been sitting on this the whole time?"

"I thought I imagined it!" Kevin shot back. "I thought if I said it, you'd all just... laugh it off. But now? After everything we've seen? The Tangles? The whispers? They knew we were coming. They've probably always known."

Amanda shook her head, eyes wide. "No. That doesn't make sense. Why would locals..."

"They're a part of *it*," Lauren whispered.

All eyes turned to her.

She stared into the fire; her face lit in flickers of orange and shadow. "They don't live near the forest. They *live in it*. They extend its reach. They are his."

Jason growled, "That's bullshit. We're just scaring ourselves."

But his voice lacked conviction, and Kevin pressed the advantage. "Think about it. The ranger practically begged us not to go in. He knew. They all know. And maybe those people on the hill weren't trying to warn us, maybe they were making sure we walked far enough in to never walk out again"

Amanda's lips parted, but no words came.

The seed of doubt had been planted.

And it rooted quickly.

That night, sleep came jagged and broken. Every time one of them shifted, the others snapped awake, certain it was something moving outside the tents.

Kevin dreamed of the hill again, of the binoculars glinting in the sun, of the hollow figures that replaced them when he blinked.

Jason lay awake with the knife across his chest, waiting for silence to fall.

Amanda whispered into her sleeping bag, counting numbers under her breath to drown out the memory of whispers.

Mark muttered curses in his dreams.

And Lauren...

Lauren listened.

It began with the heavy silence.

One moment the forest was alive, the buzz of insects, the rustle of leaves, the drip of dew from high branches.

The next, it was gone.

The hush pressed against their tents like hands. Their breathing grew loud, unbearably loud. Every shift of fabric, every scrape of skin on nylon, echoed unnaturally far.

And in that silence came the voice.

"...Lauren..."

She sat up, eyes wide, breath shallow.

The whisper slid through the air, warm and close, though no mouth had spoken it. "...Lauren... come closer..."

Her lips trembled. "Mom?"

"...yes little bird..."

Little bird, only her mother had ever called her that. She unzipped her tent with slow, shaking hands. The sound of the teeth sliding apart was thunder in the silence.

Outside, the Tangles stood.

Dozens of them, ringed around the camp, their vine-limbs creaking as they tilted their heads toward her. In the fire's last embers, their hollows glistened like eyes.

One stepped forward, smaller than the rest. Twigs woven into the suggestion of a child's form. A faint scrap of red cloth tangled in its shoulder.

Lauren covered her mouth. A sob escaped anyway.

"...not alone... never alone..."

The small figure lifted its hand as if wanting to lead her somewhere.

The voices layered, hundreds of them, all whispering at once. Some hers, some strangers, some she swore belonged to her own family though they had never stepped foot here.

She grabbed the childlike figures hand made of twigs and moss, and he led her away from the camp.

Her legs moved before she decided.

She walked past the tents. Past the fire. Into the ring of waiting Tangles.

"...come little bird..." said the Knot in her mother's voice.

And when Jason woke at dawn and unzipped her tent, he found it empty.

Only a faint trail of moss led into the trees.

She was his now.

He unwove her with care, strand by strand, until her voice tangled with his. Her fear became his root. Her memory became his doorway.

And in her memory, he found new soil.

He saw a land far to the north, where the trees were thin and pale, where snow buried their trunks in silence deeper than his own. A frozen forest, untouched and vast, where winter reigned longer than summer.

The Knot pressed himself into that place through her.

For the first time, he felt the bite of pure cold. Frost glittered on his bark, snow clung to his moss, ice seeped into his roots. And he did not wither. He thrived.

The cold sharpened him. Strengthened him. Cleansed the rot of summer.

He drank it in like fire, and when he returned to Blackwood, he was renewed.

The others still slept, still dreamed, still hoped.

But their hope was nothing.

Lauren had been the first key.

Through her, he had opened the frozen world.

Through the others, he would open every door.

And when he had taken them all, there would be no forest untouched, no city unrooted, no home unbroken.

He would spread.

He would tangle.

He would grow.

Forever.

Chapter Thirteen: Wires And Roots

Lauren's voice whispered in him, a new thread in his ever-growing weave. Through her, he had reached the frozen forests. Through her, he had tasted the purity of silence beneath snow.

But when he turned back toward the camp, he felt something strange.

A flicker.

Not the warm flicker of firelight, nor the pulse of blood in veins. This was sharper, colder, humming in stuttering bursts like sap trapped in metal veins.

One of them carried it.

The boy with the glowing screen.

The Knot did not yet understand what it was, not fully. But he recognized the pattern. Lines crisscrossed, carrying voice across distance, binding the world together as roots bound trees. A web. A lattice. A new kind of forest, not of bark and leaf, but of signal and wire.

He pressed himself closer, reaching through the silence. He could not slip through the wires, not yet. They were too narrow, too fast, too alien. His tangles had no purchase there.

But the voices. The voices traveled through. He could hear them, faintly, like whispers carried on roots deeper than the soil.

He smiled, bark creaking.

If he tangled the boy, he could follow the web. He could spread not only from tree to tree, but from screen to screen, home to home, voice to voice.

He could infest not just forests, but the entire world of men.

The Knot leaned in closer.

And the boy stirred.

Kevin pulled his phone out by instinct.

The battery had died a day ago, the screen black and useless, but he found himself clutching it anyway, thumb swiping across dead glass like muscle memory.

He sighed, pressing the dark phone against his forehead. "God, I'd kill for one more video. Just one. Any video. Doesn't even matter what. A dumb cat video. A fail compilation. Anything before I..."

He trailed off. He couldn't finish the sentence.

The silence pressed in.

And then, the screen lit up.

Kevin yelped, nearly dropping it. The glow was faint, pale, unnatural. Not the clean blue-white of a phone charging, but a sickly greenish hue, like a swamp light seen through fog.

Lines crawled across the glass, twisting, intersecting. They weren't icons. They weren't letters. They looked like... roots.

Then came the sound.

Static at first, a hiss like wind through dead leaves. Then words stretched and fractured, spilling from the speaker though the phone was off.

"...Kevin..."

His stomach dropped.

"...closer... bring me... closer..."

The voice was his own.

Kevin scrambled back, clutching the device like it was burning him. His breathing came sharp and ragged. The phone was dark again, but his ears rang with the echo.

The Knot had spoken through it.

Through the wires.

Through him.

He waited until morning before he told them.

The others looked wrecked, eyes red, faces hollow, hands trembling as they packed what little gear they had left. Jason barked orders without conviction, Amanda muttered to herself, and Mark refused to meet anyone's eyes.

Kevin swallowed hard. "I need to tell you something."

Jason shot him a glare. "What now?"

"My phone." Kevin's voice cracked. "It turned on. Last night. No battery, no service, nothing. But it lit up. And it... spoke."

Amanda's face twisted. "Spoke? You mean, you heard the whispers again."

"No." Kevin shook his head violently. "It *used my phone.* It spoke through it. Like the way it whispers through the trees. Like—like it's learning. It can use wires. Signals. All of it. And if it takes me, it won't just stay here. It'll spread. Everywhere."

Mark barked out a humorless laugh. "Great. So, the haunted bark-man is also a hacker now. Perfect."

Kevin's hands trembled. "I'm serious. That's what it wants. That's why it wants us. Because we don't just belong here. We belong everywhere. It can use us like... like keys."

The silence that followed was worse than denial.

Because they all believed him.

Jason's jaw worked, grinding against the thought. "Then we don't let it. We stick together. We don't answer the whispers. We keep moving. We get out."

Amanda crossed her arms tight. "And if we can't?"

No one answered.

They broke camp in silence, the forest pressing close around them. Each step forward felt heavier, like walking deeper into a mouth that was already chewing.

And though none of them said it aloud, the thought gnawed at every one of them:

Kevin was right.

The Knot wasn't just hunting them.

It was learning them.

And soon, it would learn the world.

Chapter Fourteen: Two Days

The Knot had learned much from the boy's device.

The wires were not roots, but they functioned the same. They connected far places. They carried voices. They hummed with unseen life, a pulse not unlike sap flowing upward from root to crown.

He pressed into it, feeling its rhythm, testing its strength. Through Kevin's pocket, he tasted the outline of a thousand other voices, places far beyond Blackwood, places of noise and light and endless wooden bones hidden beneath the walls.

But he could not pass through. Not yet. He needed Kevin inside the web of tangles, his roots wound into his veins. Only then would the pathways open.

So he waited. Patient as bark. Patient as rot.

The others were already breaking.

The fight began when Jason caught Mark slowing at the back of the line.

"Why are you slowing us down Mark?," Jason snapped, sweat pouring down his face as he hacked at a wall of creeping undergrowth.

"Slowing us down?" Mark spat, eyes wild. "Maybe I don't feel like running headlong into the next nightmare, huh? Maybe we're already dead, just like all those people on the bulletin board. Like Ethan has been for almost a year. You're just too stubborn to admit it! They're all dead Jason!"

Jason shoved him hard against a tree. "Don't you dare quit on me. We will make it out....."

Mark's knife flashed out of instinct, trembling in his hand. For a moment it looked as if one of them might drive steel into the other.

Amanda broke between them, screaming. "Stop it! Just stop it! You're both insane! We can't, we can't fight each other too!"

Her voice echoed unnaturally far. The forest had gone silent again.

Kevin froze. "It's here."

The quiet smothered them. Their ragged breathing roared in their own ears. Every heartbeat felt like a drum.

And then the Tangles appeared.

Dozens of them, sliding out from the bark of the trees themselves, their hollow eyes fixed on the campers. One moved like a marionette toward the group, vines creaking, its shape grotesque but unmistakably human.

Jason raised his knife. "Stay behind me!"

The whisper rose, hundreds of voices folding into one.

"...Jason..."

He stiffened. The knife wavered in his grip.

"...Jason... strong Jason... come closer..."

The voice was Lauren's.

Jason's eyes went wide, his breath faltered. For the first time, Kevin saw true fear crack the mask of leadership he'd worn since they had known him.

"Lauren?" His voice was small, broken.

The nearest Tangle tilted its head. Moss hung from its vine-shoulders like hair. From its hollow mouth spilled a chorus of voices, Lauren's chief among them.

"...we're safe now... Jason... join us..."

The knife fell from his hand.

Amanda screamed his name, but Jason was already stepping forward. His eyes glistened, locked on the shape before him as if hypnotized.

One more step. Another.

The vines opened.

And the forest swallowed him whole.

Amanda collapsed to her knees. Her scream cracked into sobs.

"They're gone. They're all gone. He's gone."

Kevin grabbed her arm. "Amanda, we have to move!"

She ripped free, eyes burning. "Move where, Kevin? *Where?* There's no way out! It's everywhere. It's already won!"

She stumbled back, shaking her head, tears streaking her dirt-stained face. "I can't. I can't anymore."

And she turned.

Kevin and Mark shouted after her, but she didn't answer. She walked into the trees, shoulders shaking, disappearing into the shadows without looking back.

The forest closed in behind her. Mark took off in a different direction.

And Kevin was alone.

He ran.

Branches clawed at his face, roots caught his feet, but he ran until his chest burned and his vision blurred. He didn't know where he was going. He only knew he had to move.

And then, through the trees, he saw it.

A cabin.

The ranger's cabin.

Its squat form sat half-hidden in shadow, the wood blackened with age, the roof sagging but intact. For the first time since they'd entered Blackwood, Kevin felt something like hope.

He stumbled toward it, tripping on roots, clawing his way across the clearing. His fists hammered the door, the windows, the walls.

"Help! Please! Let me in! Please, it's out here!"

His voice cracked raw against the silence.

Inside, a light flickered.

The Ranger sat in his chair with his arms on the rests. The old kerosene lamp hissed on the table beside him. The cabin walls groaned against the knocking, against the scratching that came in waves like claws raking at the timber.

He didn't move.

He'd heard it before. Too many times.

The voices outside were never the ones they seemed. Sometimes they called like children. Sometimes like lovers. Sometimes like his own.

But he knew better. He knew this was a prison for a monster.

This cabin was lined. Metal sheathing behind every board, steel bracing every doorframe. The Knot could not pass through.

The ranger lifted the bottle beside him, took a long swallow, and set it down with a hollow thud.

"I tried to warn you all," he muttered. His voice rasped in the dim light. "This stretch of forest is sour. Noone should venture these woods but, they never listen to the warnings."

The knocking grew louder. Desperate. Then fell to sobbing. Then silence.

He sat unmoving, eyes on the wall, his arms on the chair rests.

He would not open the door.

Not tonight.

Not ever.

Kevin's fists ached from pounding the cabin door. His throat was raw from screaming, his lungs burned with every sob.

But the ranger never came.

Through the tiny cracks in the barred and boarded windows, Kevin saw the faint flicker of lamplight. A silhouette sitting in stillness, unmoving, unflinching, like a statue. The shadow never rose, never wavered, even as Kevin begged and clawed at the door.

The man was in there. He knew.

And he wasn't coming.

Kevin pressed his forehead to the wood, weeping. The silence outside pressed closer, muffling even his own cries. His breath roared in his ears. His heartbeat thundered.

When the whisper came, it was not from the trees.

It came from inside his pocket.

He yanked the phone out. The screen glowed sickly, veins of pale green crawling across its black glass like roots etched in frost.

"...Kevin..."

The voice was his own. His laugh. His cry. His every word, tangled back against him.

He hurled the phone at the cabin wall. It hit with a dull crack and fell into the dirt, the screen still glowing faintly.

"No!" Kevin screamed. "You don't get me! You don't get me!"

And he ran.

The forest clawed at him, tearing skin, snapping twigs beneath his boots that echoed too far in the silence. He didn't care. He didn't look back.

He remembered the watchers.

The hill. The shapes standing in a line. The binoculars glinting in the sun.

They had to know something. They had been there since the beginning. Maybe they were survivors. Maybe they had found a way to endure where others had fallen.

They had to help him.

They had to.

His legs carried him through endless undergrowth, roots grabbing at his ankles like pleading hands. The forest seemed to lean, too close, but the hill rose ahead, pale in the moonlight.

He stumbled upward, scrambling on all fours as the slope steepened. His palms bled against the stone. His breath rasped and ragged, tore from his chest.

At the crest, he collapsed to his knees.

And there they were.

The watchers.

Five of them, standing in a line, just as before. Their outlines were human enough, tall, and broad, but they did not move. Binoculars hung from each face, glass reflecting the moon.

Kevin's chest hitched with sobs. "Please," he gasped. "Please, you've been here all along. You know. You know how to stop it. Tell me. Tell me what to do."

The silence thickened.

Then, in perfect unison, the watchers lowered their binoculars.

Kevin's heart stopped.

Behind the glass, there were no eyes. Only hollows, deep and black, where faces should have been.

The shapes were not men. Not anymore.

Their skin was bark, cracked and groaning. Their arms were latticed with vines. Their jaws unhinged, creaking wide as splinters peeled back into the shape of smiles.

The watchers stepped forward, perfectly together.

"...Kevin..."

It was his voice, all of them speaking at once.

"...we've been waiting for you..."

Kevin tried to run, but the hill betrayed him. His legs tangled in roots that hadn't been there before. His chest hit the dirt, breath knocked from him.

Hands of vine and bark reached down, curling around his wrists, his throat, his jaw. They pulled him upright as though he weighed nothing at all.

The hollows opened wider.

"...through you... the world..."

The last thing Kevin saw was his own reflection in their glass binoculars, his face pale, eyes wide, mouth screaming, before the vines forced him back, into the hollows of the watchers' bodies.

The forest closed over him.

And Kevin was tangled.

Inside the cabin, the ranger sat unmoving.

He heard the screams, carried through the silence. He heard the knocking fade, replaced by the snapping of branches and the ragged, hopeless cry of a boy who still thought the forest would show mercy.

He did not rise.

He sipped from his bottle, the kerosene lamp sputtering beside him. In the dark cabin, the ranger's eyes glowed faintly with the deep purple void fires of creation itself. He shifted his weigh tin the chair.

Something in the world had changed.

The walls groaned under phantom claws, the windows rattled with the weight of fists that weren't fists at all.

He knew better.

They always came. Always begged. Always wore voices not their own.

He had warned those kids.

Nobody ever listens.

And he was not wrong.

So he sat. And he waited.

Outside, Blackwood claimed another.

Chapter Sixteen: The Quiet Surrender

Amanda had stopped running hours ago.

The forest had taken Jason in an instant, devoured Kevin in his frenzy, and left her wandering the black maze of trunks with no sense of time or direction. Her boots dragged, her breath came shallow. She no longer cared about the trail, about the map, about escape.

The silence followed her.

At first she had fought it, clapping, stomping, forcing her voice loud just to break the suffocating hush. But the silence always won. It pressed against her skull, smothering her cries until even her own heartbeat felt borrowed.

Now she did not resist.

She trudged on until she found herself in a clearing. The moon hung pale and thin above, its light falling across a pond ringed with moss. The surface reflected her face in broken ripples: hollow-eyed, dirt-streaked, hair clinging to sweat. She looked more like the forest than herself.

Amanda sank to her knees by the water. Her shoulders trembled, but she did not cry. There were no tears left.

"It's over," she whispered. Her voice carried unnaturally far. "I'm tired. Take me. Just take me already."

The forest answered with silence.

And then with whispers.

"...Amanda..."

She did not flinch.

"...no more running... no more fighting... rest..."

The voices overlapped, soft and endless, wrapping around her like roots around stone.

"...we will carry you... you will never be alone..."

She closed her eyes.

For the first time since stepping into Blackwood, her body loosened. She leaned forward, letting her weight carry her over the pond. Icy water swallowed her face, her chest, her limbs. She let it take her, let the moss wrap around her wrists, let the vines curl around her ankles.

When she sank into the roots below, she did not fight.

And Amanda was gone.

The Knot unwove her gently.

Unlike Jason, who resisted with his pride, or Kevin, who thrashed with his fear, Amanda came willingly. She loosened her own threads, and he tangled them into himself without struggle.

Her despair was sweet. Her exhaustion, pure. She did not resist the silence; she embraced it. And so she became silent, another voice layered into his chorus, another root spreading from his trunk.

Through her, he found something new.

The cities.

The crowded places of glass and metal where she had lived her whole life. She had called them safe, called them home, though the trees there were fewer, choked between streets. But still, they were there, lining boulevards, pressed into furniture, hidden in beams behind plaster.

Wood was everywhere.

Through Amanda, he tasted it.

Every doorframe. Every chair. Every desk, table, and floorboard. He saw a thousand pathways opening, each one a vein leading into the heart of their civilization.

And he realized how fragile it truly was.

They thought themselves beyond him, shielded by steel, by glass, by concrete. But wood was their foundation, their skeleton. The same substance they cut from his forest, the same roots they burned without thought, was the same substance that held their world together.

Through Amanda, he could reach it.

He was no longer bound to Blackwood.

The frozen forest through Lauren. The wire-web through Kevin. The cities through Amanda.

The mountains and deserts through Jason

Four keys.

He needed only the last.

Mark, rootless and bitter. A branch without soil. His despair would open the forgotten places, the wastelands and roadsides, the corners of the world where silence had already reigned.

The Knot stirred.

He was close now.

So very close.

Chapter Seventeen: The Bitter Branch

Mark had always told himself he didn't care. Even before the forest. Even before the Tangles and the whispers. Back in the city, back in the half-empty apartment with its peeling paint and overdue bills, Mark had lived by one rule: don't get attached. Don't expect anyone to stay. Don't expect anything to last.

Because it never did.

Jobs came and went. Friends drifted. Family stopped calling. When Jason invited him on this trip, Mark only said yes because Jason had been the one friend that didn't leave.

Now, with Jason gone, Amanda gone, Kevin gone, Lauren gone... the rule had proved itself again.

He was alone.

And the silence agreed.

Mark staggered through the trees, knife clutched in one hand, his other arm wrapped tight across his ribs. His breaths came ragged, tearing at his throat. He didn't know how long he had been walking. Hours. Days. The forest did not measure time in ways men understood.

The silence followed him like a shadow.

Every so often, he would stop and shout. He would curse the trees, curse the ranger who had locked himself away, curse Jason for dragging them here. His voice always carried too far, echoing in the muffled air until he hated the sound of it.

And the whispers always came.

"...Mark..."

"...you don't belong... you never belonged..."

He snarled back at them his voice breaking. "Shut up! You don't know me!"

But they did.

"...rootless branch... no soil... no home..."

He dropped to his knees, knife slipping from his hand. His shoulders shook, not with fear but with laughter, dry, hollow, desperate. "Yeah," he whispered. "Yeah, that's me."

The Tangles emerged from the trees.

They formed a circle around him, moving with patient unity. Their hollows glistened in the moonlight, their vine-limbs twitching like nerves. One leaned forward, its form broad-shouldered, knife-shaped twig clenched in its hand, an echo of Jason.

Another tilted its head, hair of moss trailing, Amanda's outline.

A third limped slightly, red cloth snagged in its bark, Kevin's shadow.

Mark looked up at them, laughter cracking into sobs. "You all left me. Every damn one of you. And now you're back."

The whispers rose in a chorus.

"...never left... never alone... be tangled with us..."

For the first time in years, Mark felt wanted.

He spread his arms wide, chest heaving. "Fine. Take me. If this is what it takes to belong... take me."

The Tangles closed in.

Vines curled around his arms, his throat, his chest. They pulled him upright, lifted him into the air as if presenting him to the forest itself. The silence deepened until his last cry echoed back at him, warped into a hundred voices.

Then the bark split open, and the Knot drew him in.

Mark was unmade.

And the Bitter Branch became part of the tree.

Inside the cabin the lamp sputtered low, casting thin shadows against the cabin walls. The ranger sat in his chair, unmoving.

He had not moved in hours. But his eyes had not closed. He knew his time here was short. Something had changed.

The forest was louder tonight. Not in sound, in hunger.

He could feel it pressing against the metal-lined walls, pressing through the cracks of the world itself. Blackwood had always taken, always whispered, always fed. But never like this. Never with this much weight.

He had seen whole groups vanish before. He had heard their cries. But this time it felt different.

The forest wasn't satisfied.

It wanted more.

And he knew, in his bones, in his blood, that it was getting stronger.

He thought of the kids, their tired faces, the desperation in their eyes when he told them, 'Two days.' He had hoped, foolishly, that they might heed his warning, turn back before it was too late.

But no one ever did.

Now they were gone. All of them. Tangled. Consumed.

The ranger stared into the sputtering flame, void fire behind his eyes.

"They'll never listen," he muttered to the silence. "Not until it's too late. And by then, it won't just be Blackwood."

Outside, something dragged across the cabin walls, claws, roots, hands. Scratching. Knocking. Testing.

The ranger closed his eyes, letting the sound wash over him. He would not answer. He never answered.

But for the first time in years, a sliver of doubt crept into his chest.

Because the forest had never sounded this hungry before.

Chapter Eighteen: The World will Become Blackwood

He had them all now.

Five threads, woven into his endless body, each one a key, each one a door.

Jason, the traveler of mountains. His strength opened paths through stone and barren heights. Where roots had once found no purchase, now they could burrow, splitting rock, weaving through canyons, spiraling upward into peaks.

Amanda, the city-dweller. Through her despair, he drank in the crowded towers of men. Wood hidden beneath concrete and steel revealed itself to him. Beams, doors, tables, chairs — all waiting. He could taste their weakness, the way their civilization leaned unknowingly upon his bones.

Lauren, the quiet one of the coldest forests of the North. Through her veins flowed the memory of birches and endless snow. She was his frost, his silence sharpened into ice. He stretched into tundra and taiga, roots cracking permafrost, branches weighted with eternal snow. For the first time, he felt winter as strength.

Kevin, the wired boy. His restless pulse was tethered to a lattice of voices and signals. Through him, the Knot discovered the echo of roots not in soil but in light and wire, crossing continents at the speed of thought. He could not yet walk those paths, but he could whisper through them. And whispers were always enough.

Mark, the bitter one. The drifter. Through him, the Knot seeped into forgotten places, the roadsides where weeds grew through cracks, the abandoned houses with their rotting beams, the dust, the sand, and the silence where no one else looked. He was the branch without soil, and so he spread into places without roots.

Together, they were complete.

Together, they were his map of the world.

The Knot breathed.

And the world shivered.

Blackwood spread.

It began at the edges of the forest. Roots thickened, splitting asphalt roads that had once carried campers and cars. Trees bent and groaned, their branches tangling until no path remained. The old signs that marked trails rotted away in an instant, wood devoured and remade into his body.

But it did not stop there.

Through Jason, the Knot stretched into the mountains. Scree and shale shifted as roots curled between them, splitting stone. Alpine woods thickened where none had grown in centuries. Snowmelt carried his seed farther down into valleys, where they sprouted in silence overnight.

Through Amanda, he reached the cities. Apartment beams groaned as moss crept between plaster. Doors warped in their frames. Floors buckled beneath invisible roots. Cabinets sprouted leaves. Furniture twisted into grotesque shapes. The people who lived there touched wood every day without knowing it, and through those touches, he whispered. And when they listened, they would tangle.

Through Lauren, the north cracked open. Frost-bitten forests awakened under his hand, ice groaning as it spread like veins through the earth. Snowdrifts whispered in voices that carried for miles silence upon silence, until even the frozen wasteland belonged to him.

Through Kevin, he flickered through wires. Not whole, not fully, but enough. Enough to carry voices into glowing screens. Enough to turn dead glass green with his pulse. Enough to remind the world that their connection was his connection. Their lattice was his lattice. Every signal hummed like a buried root waiting to sprout.

Through Mark, he bled into deserts, into ruins, into forgotten corners where silence had already reigned. Abandoned motels sprouted vines through cracked beams. Old roadside diners groaned as their signs toppled into tangles of moss. The places no one remembered became his first.

The Knot stretched, and Blackwood stretched with him.

For the first time, he was not bound to one forest.

For the first time, the world itself was his body.

Wood. Wire. Ice. Steel. Sand. Stone.

All of it was soil. All of it was root.

All of it was Blackwood.

The infestation that called itself man would wither. Their civilization would crack. Their

homes, their roads, their cities would be tangled,
reclaimed, unwoven.

Because there had only ever been one truth.

The earth was not theirs.

It had always been his.

And now the Knot would remind them.

Forever.

Chapter Nineteen: The Five Keys

They had fought.
They had run.
They had begged.

But now they were tangled, unwoven, and remade.

Five keys. Five Doors. Five roots sunk deep into the earth.

The Knot had broken them apart carefully, pulling threads of flesh, fear, and memory, then weaving them anew from vine, bark, and silence. But unlike the others he had collected over the centuries, these five were not left hollow.

He had awakened them.

And they had accepted.

Jason stood first. His body was a lattice of muscle and root, his shoulders broad, his knife-arm replaced by a jagged branch sharper than steel. Where once he had led his friends, now he would lead the hunt. His voice was stone breaking:

"I will carve the mountains for you. I will open the high places."

Amanda rose next. Moss draped her shoulders like a cloak; her hollowed eyes gleamed with city lights. Her mouth split into a wooden smile. Her voice carried the echo of subway tunnels:

"I will whisper through the walls. Through beams and doors. Through every home."

Lauren stepped forward slowly, frost clinging to her bark-skin, her hair a cascade of pale lichen. Her voice was soft as if carried on a light snowfall gently falling through the air.

"I will spread the cold. The frozen places will open to you. Ice will not hold us back."

Kevin followed, his chest glowing faintly, wires running like veins through his vine-flesh, his bark fingers sparking with unnatural energy. His voice stuttered in overlapping echoes, as though carried on static:

"I will crawl the wires. The screens will glow with your voice. They will listen, and they will tangle."

Mark came last, bitter even in rebirth, his body twisted in knots of thorn and rot. He dragged one leg as though broken, but where he walked, weeds sprouted from dead earth. His voice was rust and dust:

"I will open the forgotten places. The ruins. The deserts. The silence lying in wait. All will be yours."

The Knot looked upon them and felt hunger turn to triumph.

They were no longer Jason, Amanda, Lauren, Kevin, or Mark.

They were his branches, his lieutenants, his roots in the wide world. Through them, his voice would carry farther. Through them, his reach would not only grow but his reach would be expedited as if a curse or a wild disease were loosed upon the world out of rage and fury.

The world thought itself safe in its cities, its deserts, its mountains, its frozen tundra, its endless wires. But every corner had been claimed now.

The Five Keys had unlocked the earth.

And they did not resist.

They welcomed their place.

Together, they spoke in one voice, a chorus of stone, steel, ice, wire, and rot:

"Cleanse. Unweave. Grow."

The Knot smiled through them.

The infestation called humanity would not be burned away in war or swept aside in fire. No. It would be *consumed from within.*

Civilization would become roots. Homes would become hollows. The world would become Blackwood.

And through his five apostles, the Knot would spread like madness.

Like plague.

Like forever.

Chapter Twenty: The Silence Beyond

The Knot was patient.

He had always been patient.

Roots did not rush, and the trees had no need to hurry. The forest had waited for centuries while men came and went, setting fires, raising cabins, cutting, and building. Believing they were the masters of the earth.

But the forest remembered. And the forest endured.

Now, at last, he had his five keys, and whatever force bound him to this forest would hold him in place no longer.

Jason, Amanda, Lauren, Kevin, and Mark. They stood at his sides, hollowed yet whole, tangled yet awakened. Not prey, not mere echoes. They were his branches now; his hands and his eyes stretched across the earth.

Through them, he would spread.

He savored their memories, each one a doorway.

Jason's climbs across jagged peaks. His blood and sweat on granite cliffs. Now every mountain was known to the Knot, every path upward a channel for roots to grow. Where man thought himself untouchable, the forest would claw its way skyward.

Amanda's crowded city streets. Her footsteps echoing in apartments built of cut beams and polished floors. Through her he tasted the heart of their civilization, the hidden veins of wood beneath plaster and stone. All those towers leaned unknowingly on him. And now he would lean back.

Lauren's frozen childhood. The crunch of snow, the endless pale silence of the northern woods. Through her veins he stretched into the tundra, into places where fire could not touch him. Winter would not be an enemy, but a cradle. A respite. Safe.

Kevin's restless pulse of light. His hands always on screens, his eyes locked on glowing windows. Through him, the Knot discovered wires were just another form of root, another web of connection. Not soil, but still a path. Through Kevin, his whispers would crawl unseen across continents.

Mark's bitterness, his drifting. The ruins, the deserts, the abandoned places he had called familiar. Through him, the Knot found every forgotten corner of the world already half-dead and waiting. He would not need to fight there. He would only need to finish what man had started.

Five keys. Five memories. Five doorways.

They were not simply his trophies, they were his map. His plague. His destiny.

Soon, he would unspool them into the world. They would walk as themselves, but not themselves. They would go home. They would open doors. They would spread his roots in silence and shadow. And everywhere they touched, Blackwood would grow.

Homes would darken.
Cities would bend.
Mountains would crack.
Ice would deepen.
Wires would hum.
Deserts would bloom with tangles.

The infestation called man would not even realize the cleansing had begun until the silence was already inside them, until their voices were already his, until their bodies were already hollowed and remade.

The Knot had no need to rush.

He had been since the first tree. He would be until the last.

Now the world would remember that truth.

Because all earth was forest. And all forest was Blackwood. And Blackwood was the Knot tying everything together.

He stretched his limbs across the night, branches arching wide, roots curling deeper, tangles whispering in chorus. His five apostles knelt at his side, waiting for the command.

But in the distance somewhere out of his sight there was a cold building. This was not the cold of the Tundra and forests of the North. It was an unnatural cold as if not from this world, and it was spreading. He looked to the sky, and from it, a sickly green burst of light shot across the sky.

The Knot could feel it encroaching from a place just outside of his reach even with the five keys. He contemplated on his next move and when to make it. Now? No...... the trees are patient.

Not yet.

Soon.

He would savor this moment, the breath before the silence. The pause before the cleansing.

When he rose, the world would not fall with fire and ruin.

It would fall with silence.

And when silence reigned, forever, the Knot would stand.

Waiting.

Growing.

Smiling.

Part 2
The Pale Hell

Chapter One: Waking in the Cold Hell

The fire had finished its work.

Lucas Cain's world was ash and smoke, the screams of his family still echoing in his ears as he dropped to his knees outside the charred remains of his home. The sirens had come too late, as they always did. And now, hollow, and empty, he let the heat of grief turn to ice.

He raised his hands, and there was nothing left to hold onto. Nothing to save. Nothing to forgive. The only path left is to end it all.

Blam!

Then came the darkness.

It wasn't like falling. Not like sleep. Not like death. It was a void that pressed against every fiber of his being, cold, sterile, and patient. The weight of it pushed the last breath from his lungs before he realized he was no longer breathing.

When Lucas opened his eyes, he was standing on what felt like a smooth sheet of ice. A gray fog swirled around him, and the smell made him retch, damp, decayed, and tangibly sickly. The ground beneath his feet felt wet, yet it didn't stain. Something in him recognized the smell as the exhalation of a million lost souls.

He tried to scream, but no sound came. He bent over, clawing at the mist that filled his lungs.

And then he heard it.

A voice. Smooth. Polished. Human, but not.

"Welcome back," it said.

Lucas turned sharply. The figure standing before him was unnervingly ordinary. A man in a tailored suit, cane in hand, glowing red eyes fixed on him. The glow was faint, like embers barely kept alive beneath frost. Yet it burned through Lucas's chest.

"Who, what..." he began.

"I am nothing you need to understand," the man said. "Yet everything you need to obey. You are in Hell, though not the kind sung in fearful songs. This is cold. Sick. Deadly."

"Do you mind if I sit?" Said the well-dressed man. Then he sat down in a chair that wasn't there as if nothing was out of the ordinary.

Lucas's knees buckled, but he did not fall. Something in his gut propelled him forward.

"Why me?" he rasped. "Why..."

"You made a choice," the man interrupted. "One of despair, one of irrevocable pain. You are mine now, Cain. And I have a proposition."

Lucas laughed bitterly. "A proposition? My family," His voice cracked. "They burned alive while I, while I *watched!* What proposition could you possibly offer me?"

The man tilted his head, cane tapping the gray mist. "Power. Vengeance. Purpose. I offer you an alternate path. You may walk the earth again if you'd like. But this time you will be indestructible, with wings that obey your will. You will be able to use these razor drawings on your skin as weapons, manifest them as an extension of yourself."

Lucas's mind flinched, heart tightening. Wings. Wire. The words felt like poison and promise all at once.

"And what do you want in return?" he asked.

"Your obedience," the figure said simply. "Your mission is simple: sow chaos. Tear the world apart. Open the barrier between this realm and Hell. Make them one."

Lucas's chest burned, not with fear, but with anticipation. He thought of the fire, of the smoke, of the smell of his family's flesh. The smell of gunpowder burned his memory. He thought of the void he'd just left. And he realized he did not need persuasion.

"I accept," he said, voice low but final.

The Devil smiled. Slowly, he extended a hand. Lucas stared, then gripped it.

"That wasn't so hard now was it?"

The handshake was fire and ice all at once. Pain lanced through his arm, and when it passed, the imprint remained, a black sigil burned into his palm, coiling like a wire-bound serpent: the Mark of Satan.

Lucas flexed his fingers. The mark burned faintly, as if alive. And for the first time since the fire, something *moved* inside him.

Wings unfurled in his back, skeletal at first, then feathered with rusted metal and frost. His arm split open along the inked wire tattoo, strands of living wire slithering across the floor, obeying his mental commands. The fog around him started to dissipate and he could see the ground clearly. The floor looked like a sheet of black marble with a layer of frost on top.

The Devil's eyes glowed brighter. "Now," he said, "the game begins."

Lucas clenched his fists. Every memory of his past life, grief, rage, helplessness, became fuel. The first step into the cold world was no step at all; it was a leap into vengeance incarnate.

Around him, the sea of shambling souls watched silently. Some moaned. Some clawed at the gray mist, hopeless, useless. None would stop him. None would matter.

The world, this world, and the one he would return to, was his canvas now. And Lucas Cain, once a man, was the harbinger of its unraveling.

The frost hissed, the wire twined, the wings flexed.

Hell was cold, and Lucas was its storm let loose.

Chapter Two: Rising From Ash and Earth

After a brief moment of numbness the first thing Lucas Cain felt was the dirt. Cold and hard. Then he opened his eyes to the darkness. Fumbling in the dark

he felt the walls of his coffin. Cheap wood splintered from the weight of the dirt above.

After collecting his thoughts and remembering the handshake with the well-dressed man in the cold place, he started to dig. Clawing his way out of the grave his body had called home for the past 3 months.

Lucas Cain fought against the dirt and wood until he burst out of the grave and with him came the frost. He noticed it immediately when his hand touched the grass on top of the grave.

The grass turned brittle and frozen on contact.

After climbing out of his own grave Lucas kneeled down in the frozen grass and breathed in and let out a primal scream until all the air left his lungs.

Lucas Cain stood up and turned to the headstone.

LUCAS CAIN

Beloved Husband and Father.

Lost too soon

1982-2025

He paused for a moment to take in the cheap headstone the city provided already crumbling to the weather. He thought of tearing it out of the ground but instead decided to carve a message into it instead.

The Harrow has Risen

The Harrow. Something inside him solidified the title.

I am The Harrow. Lucas Cain is no more.

After carving the headstone he turned around, and an icy pain shot through his body bringing him to his knees.

The wings started protruding out of his back. At first it was the bones and from the bone structure of the wings, feathers formed, made of steel and rust. The wings finished forming and the smell of rust filled the air around him.

Then the pain shot through his forearms. He pulled his arms up in front of his eyes and then he saw it. The razor wire tattoos writhing under his skin and starting to protrude from his arms like snakes in the sand.

He stared in awe at the manifestation of the razor wires coming from his forearms.

"These will come in handy" he said as the razor wire tattoos sprang to life. And then he heard it. Footsteps approaching.

"If anybody is out here with messing with my cemetery there is going to be hell to pay you little- "the grave keeper stopped before he finished the sentence.

'Hell to pay' thought The Harrow and chuckled to himself. What a choice of words.

Without giving the grave keeper time to fully take in what he was seeing Lucas extended his wings and took off into the night sky leaving the grave keeper stunned.

With the wind whooshing by his ears and through his wings Lucas was ready to start.

Chapter Three: The Detective

Andre Voss had seen his fair share of nasty things the world had to offer. Murder. Rape. Bombs falling out of the sky during the war. But he had never seen anything like the scene before him.

It was 3 am when he arrived at St. Andrew's Cemetery right outside of town. The wind carried an unnatural chill that bit through his overcoat, cutting straight to the bone. The cemetery was silent except for the faint creak of tree limbs overhead, each one rimed in frost.

Voss's boots crunched through a crust of ice that shouldn't have been there. It was slick beneath his feet, and his breath puffed white into the air.

The grave keeper, a bitter old man, called in and was babbling on about the man with the rusted wings. But the part that made Voss' heart skip a beat was the grave that the old man was babbling about.

Lucas Cain.

His partner had shot himself after the arsonist set his house ablaze with his family inside. Gone too soon. Voss was a God-fearing man, and he knew that suicide was a one-way ticket to the fires of hell.

What he did not know was that Hell is not what they sell you in Sunday school. Fire. Brimstone. Little demons with pitch forks and bifurcated tails.

No, Hell was cold, rusted, and sick. Frosted over. Endless and unforgiving.

He finished his cigarette and flicked it into the unnatural frost beneath his feet.

He looked into the open grave. It did not appear to be dug into but out of as if something burst out of it. The unnatural frost covered everything. This wouldn't normally concern him except it's the middle of July. Winter was nowhere near rearing its cold unforgiving face.

Voss stood at the edge of the grave scanning everything to look for clues but inside he knew. Somehow he just knew what happened.

"What did you do Lu? Why is this happening in my lifetime?" He whispered under his breath.

After taking in the empty grave and the unnatural frost that surrounded it he saw the markings.

The Harrow has Risen

Reading this in his head sent chills down his spine and his body shuddered. This did not sit well with Voss. Not at all.

But where can this investigation go from here with this outlandish information provided by the crime scene? Who should he report this too? His Boss? Knowing the chief he would say something about just some punks and their viral pranks or something and then dismiss the case.

A priest felt like a more fitting direction, but what would they do? Seven hail Mary's and you're good? Doubtful.

This was ominous indeed and gave off a sense of urgency.

He needed to get moving.

With that, detective Voss lit another cigarette and headed toward his cruiser.

Chapter Four: Wings and Wires

With the wind whipping through his rusted wings, The Harrow soared through the sky. A Predator. He scanned the city streets below him looking for his first victim.

He knew the area, and he knew where to look for his first target.

East Side. The slums were fraught with danger. Drug dealers. Thieves. Murderers.

He knew of an abandoned warehouse that was a main 'exchange' place for drug deals and weapons tradeoffs.

When the warehouse was in sight he circled above looking for a place to land.

Just before he landed on the busted roof of the building he saw the flicker of headlights turning into the remains of what was once a parking lot for employees. Not one but three blacked out SUVs pulled in one right after the other.

The SUVs pulled around and parked near the building side by side. He watched the men exit the vehicles.

Sagging pants and green bandannas. These men belonged to the gang that ran the lower east side. He had dealt with them before. That was when he got shot for the first time. A routine traffic stop turned shooting.

The men were armed with pistols and a couple of them had AK-47s. They looked anxious like they didn't trust who they were meeting. Fidgeting and inspecting their weapons.

The flicker of headlights cut through the dark once again and two cars on rims pulled in and parked facing the armed men in the parking lot. Five men exited the two vehicles and stood a small distance away from the heavily armed group.

The Harrow watched the two groups interacting. He heard someone mention a drop and another was asking where the money is. Just as things started to escalate to the heated argument stage, The Harrow decided it was time to crash the party.

With a flurry of metal and frost The Harrow ascended into the night sky and dive bombed the group landing in between the two groups in a classic 'superhero' landing. His rusted wings scraped the ground as he slowly stood.

The two groups were stunned and stood there in a confused state trying to process what just happened.

"How's business going fellas?" The Harrow mocked.

"What the f- "started one of the men before his neck started gushing blood from the razor wire that just ripped his throat out.

Then came the gunfire thundering through the stillness of the night. Lucas stood and laughed at the wasted bullets and continued to tear through the group. He found his wings served as useful weapons after grabbing one of the men with his razor wire extensions and slicing him in half vertically, so everything spilled out onto the now frost covered concrete.

Two of the men threw up at the grotesque sight.

"Running will not save you....." Lucas growled at the men in a voice not of this world. A hungry voice.

The men were frozen where they stood. 'Is this really happening?' they all thought to themselves as The Harrow walked towards them all. Frost spider-webbing from his every step.

The Harrow is among us. And the frost is his wake.

Chapter Five: The First Wireborn

Father Aurek had been with the church over on the east side for a long time. His eyes have seen too many funerals for too many that were taken too soon. The liquor helped him most nights. He had spent time in the drunk tank recently on a public intoxication charge.

That was 2 days ago.

Today was Thursday and that meant helping the volunteers hand out sandwiches at the community center. Somewhat easy day. Unless of course one of the drunk ones show up and start their crap again. His faith in this city recuperating from the recent loss, had been lost.

The fancy skyscraper in North town had befallen a terrorist attack and fell. That took out five and a half city blocks. Where all the fancy stores were. The billionaire who owned it talked badly about someone he probably shouldn't have.

"Alright everybody we gotta get ready to close up shop!" Father Aurek announced in his low booming voice.

He turned and started to say something to one of the volunteers and then it happened. A drunk one. It was Damen again. He had been directly affected by the collapse of the skyscraper. His store was one of the ones that got smashed.

That store had his life savings wrapped up into it. But he didn't have enough for insurance. He planned to get it, but he was waiting to turn a profit from the store. 'Poor guy' Thought

Father Aurek. At the door, the altercation was intensifying.

"Don't fucking touch me you bastards!" Shouted Damen at the volunteer trying to keep him under control and outside the building.

"Damnit Damen!" Father Aurek boomed.

"Don't be bringing that nonsense around here again son. I'll be more than happy to knock some sense into you!"

Father Aurek's booming voice only intensified the conflict.

Damen reached into his jacket and pulled out a knife, but he held it as though scared to actually use it. Father Aurek stepped forward with his hands up trying to calm the man down again.

"Alright Damen this is not necessary son" he said in a slightly gentler tone.

"No you don't understand Father. I lost everything. I'll never recover from that tower falling. I have nothing to lose" Damen blubbered holding tears back.

"What exactly do you intend to do here son? There's no money here, you know that."

"I'm not here for money Father." His voice turned cold and almost autonomous. His expression changed from that of a scared child to man with cruel intent.

Damen produced a pistol from his jacket with his free hand. His hands not terrified of the gun or the knife anymore. Father Aurek's eyes widened but he leapt into action trying to grab the gun and during the struggle the gun went off.

Lucas Cain had been flying past the community center merely going to his next target. The crooked cop. Jonathan Vaughn.

He was known to the city as a hero.

The Harrow knew better.

'Jon Von' they called him at the station. He was a ruthless man with a saintly smile that instantly won people over. The life of the party. Boogeyman to some.

A while back Lucas Cain the detective was hot on his trail of lies, extortion, murder, and trafficking ring. And now The Harrow is picking up the pace.

Blam!

Blam!

The Harrow heard the gunshots before he saw the commotion. It was the community center where he had helped Father Aurek hand food out from time to time. He dove down and landed in the street outside the center, leaving a small crater that looked like a bomb made of frost went off.

He ran through the doorway and saw Father Aurek still struggling with the gunman. The Harrow reached out with his wires slicing the young man's hands off immediately. Before Damen's hands hit the floor The Harrow already had him wrapped up in his wires. The frost emanated from The Harrow and his extensions.

"Lucas?" asked Father Aurek "How? What is going on?!?"

The Harrow turned to the priest as he ripped the man is his grasp apart in a swift motion. Blood sprayed everywhere. The cafeteria and everyone in it were now covered with the man's blood.

"Yes Father it's me. But better." he responded to the stunned priest.

"I have been sent back from the cold hell, and I bring with me a frost that will take everything from everyone. Just like that psycho did to me." the Harrow was not only talking to Father Aurek now but every witness he had before him.

"I have been sent back to destroy, to sow chaos. I am the frost of Hell. I give you two options... You follow and help sow the chaos and plant the wires. Nurture the frost with your disregard for the world." The Harrow paused, "or perish..."

He turned to Father Aurek, and he glided across the floor, carried by frost. He reached out to the priests clutched arm where blood was dripping down.

"Move your hand Father." He stated

"What are you going to do to me?" the priest asked. Not scared but curious.

Their eyes met. In a daze as if hypnotized the priest slowly removed his arm. The Harrow reached out with his hand and touched the wound uniting the priest with the frost of Hell.

The pain seared through every region of his body. He flinched at the pain, but no sound escaped his lips. When Father Aurek opened his eyes he saw the razor wire tendrils retracting from his wound. But the frost lingered.

It was part of him now.

He had become the first Wireborn. It was at that moment Lucas Cain knew what needed to be done to fulfill his promise to the well-dressed man in the cold place. Recruitment. And one by one the volunteers knelt before him to receive the gift of frost.

The Harrow leads us.

Chapter Six: The Fire

Detective Lucas Cain had just finished wrapping up paperwork at the office with his partner Andre Voss. They had finally closed a murder case that kept them busy for the past couple months. Following leads that lead only to dead ends, stakeouts with no results. Rinse and repeat.

Bu they finally got a break in the case 2 days ago when the killer crashed a stolen car and had been knocked unconscious. Lucky break was all it chocked up to.

The two worn out detectives gathered their things and headed home.

"See ya tomorrow Lu." Voss said as he pushed the door open and stepped out into the world outside.

"Yep, see ya tomorrow Voss." He replied

Lucas Cain was headed toward the door when his phone rang. It was his wife again. Probably to see if he is coming home soon.

"Hey Lady." He said in a loving tone.

Only silence answered him.

"Maryam? Is everything alright?" he questioned.

Silence.

"Hello detective Cain." Responded the voice. But it wasn't his wife's voice.

"Do you remember me?" asked the man.

Detective Cain recognized the voice and his heart sank. The voice belonged to a serial arsonist that him and Voss put away years ago. There's no way he should be out of prison. Jack

Long had been sentenced to 10 years. But that was only 5 years ago.

"What are doing on my wife's phone Jack?" Lucas asked his grip tightening on his phone.

"I told you and Detective Voss I would come back. You haven't been watching the news lately have you detective?" Jack asked.

"No I have not. Where is my family?" he asked, anger slipping through his voice.

"I found a way out of the facility 3 days ago and now I am at your house. Detective Voss doesn't really have much to lose. But you? You have so very, very much to lose." Said the man on the phone ending the sentence with a taunting hiss.

"Don't you Dare..." Lucas started.

"It's already started Detective!" the arsonist interrupted. "You won't make it in time. Especially not since the fire was set 30 minutes ago and the house went up spectacularly. Your families screams were music to my ears."

Detective Lucas Cain ran to his car and sped towards his home. He could see the smoke. No. Please no. Not this. Not now.

He arrived before the firetrucks, but he could hear them in the distance. Too late. The house was burning, and he could feel his family was no longer with him. He stepped out of the car and looked at the blaze, the fire flickering in his eyes.

Lucas Cain dropped to his knees and let out a primal scream.

"NOOOO!!!"

His phone started ringing. It was Voss. He clicked the side button to reject the call. It rang again. Rejected.

Lucas was done here. He pulled his gun from its holster for the last time. The blaze reflected off the shiny surface of the pistol. Standard issue. Nothing special.

Lucas raised the gun to his head and pulled the trigger.

LUCAS CAIN
Beloved Husband and Father.
Lost too soon
1982-2025

He was done with this world... For now.

Chapter Seven: Perspective

The Devil sat on his throne in front of the vision pool that let him observe the world above. This was supposed to be a punishment. To see a world he can't touch. Just a viewer. But he was now using this punishment as a tool to let him see the progress of his Harrow.

He had his cane laid across his lap with his legs crossed. He had watched as his Harrow ripped those gangsters to shreds. Putting his new abilities to good use. Then there was the man from the community center.

Now Father Aurek. A man of God. He succumbed to the frost without hesitation. As if he had given up on the God he preached about throughout his entire life.

The first Wireborn. And with Father Aurek came the congregation he preached to. Some took convincing but most accepted the frost.

Father Aurek set into motion the initiation of the Wireborn. This initiation consisted of kneeling before Father Aurek while the rest of the congregation sang an odd hymn.

"Stillness to flesh, frost to blood... Bone to sky, rust to wing... Harrow, Harrow, make the world still..."

The new initiate that knelt in front of Father Aurek as he finished his initiation speech. He was nervous. He had seen the other initiate killed in front of him for making a sound during the crowning of razor wire.

Father Aurek lifted the razor wire crown above the initiate's head and began to lower it onto his head. The pain seared through his scalp. He held back a scream. He wanted to belong to the frost.

Father Aurek twisted the crown onto the initiate's head and turned to reach into the birdbath where they kept the frost used for the initiation. He dipped his hand in and scooped some out and sprinkled the frost onto the initiate's head.

The fresh wounds drank up the frost. And then he felt it. The frost coursing through his veins. He had become Wireborn. He felt the slight surge of strength shoot through his muscles. The frost comes with power.

The Devil watched this unfold through the window to the world above. The Harrow had started off with a bang. 4 days and you have the start of a cult already? Impressive he thought while fidgeting with his cane.

The Devil rose from his frosted throne and began circling the icy oval window to the world above. Contemplating. Planning.

The world will be defeated, and the Harrow will see it through to its inevitable end. In the background from the icy window he could hear the Wireborn start another Hymn.

"The cold does not forgive...
The cold does not yield...
I am the edge of the frost...
the shadow of the breach...
the hand of the Frostfather in the warm world."

The Devil listened to the Hymn. Replaying it in his head.

"The cold does not forgive...
The cold does not yield...

I am the edge of the frost...

the shadow of the breach...

the hand of the Frostfather in the warm world."

He continued pacing and listening to the Hymns of the Wireborn.

Th Devil smiled showing his too perfect teeth.

Chapter Eight: The Frostline

The frostline was not a fence or a wall. It was a change in the air, colder, sharper, as if each breath had a blade in it. The snow here was different too, not white but a faint, luminous blue. It started shortly after The Harrow got his first kill.

It started in St. Andrew's Cemetery at the Harrow's grave. The heat from the summer had no effect on the snow or the frost. The frost taunted the heat from the summer day.

Police tape still lingered around the part of the cemetery where Lucas Cain's grave stood. Open like a wound in the earth.

The grave keeper avoided that part of the cemetery all together after the incident. But something was off today. He stumbled up to the far part of the cemetery where the winged man's grave sat, still open.

What concerned him the most was the frost. It is July, frost should not be on the list of things to worry about. But there it was. Emanating from the open grave as if someone left the door open on a snowy day.

When the grave keeper got to the far end of the cemetery he noticed how the air changed. He felt the frosted knives in the air he breathed. This cold did not belong to this world.

As he stood there shivering, something shot out of the hole and landed on the snow-covered ground before his feet. Above him the sky flashed a sickly green hue that stretched out across the sky.

"What in the world is this?" he asked under his breath.

He picked up the object and studied it. It seemed to be a chain, but it was made of bone. Each link fused together, and each were etched with words in a language no one alive could fully translate.

The object felt wrong as if it wasn't supposed to be here. The grave keeper tossed the object to the ground.

The old man scurried off towards his cabin cursing the frost. Crunch. Crunch. Crunch.

A relic of the frost had been put into play. The Harrow felt it's presence and took flight. He was being pulled to it. This was a gift from the well-dressed man in the frozen Hell. He would accept this gift and use it to spread the frost.

When The Harrow arrived at his grave and landed with a loud thump that was slightly muffled by the thick layer of snow and frost. He stood up and scanned the ground feeling for the objects location.

Then he saw it. A link of chains constructed of bone fused together etched with what seemed to be a language foreign to him but familiar to the frost. He picked the object up and the words changed from the foreign language to plain English. His fingers brushed the links, and frost crawled across the bones in spiderweb patterns.

It read as follows:

This chain is the chain that binds the breach.

When this chain breaks, the breach has opened.

Use this chain to pass the message of the breach.

The Wireborn will worship and protect this relic of the frost.

The Harrow clutched the object. He will take this to Father Aurek. Aurek will see to it that it is kept safe while The Harrow works.

The first Relic of the frost had been given to the Harrow.

The Chain that binds will break.

The Harrow will make sure of that.

Chapter Nine: Heaven's Hand

Detective Voss had kept to himself after losing his partner. He found little comfort in the bottle of whiskey beside him. They had worked so well together despite their rocky start. Lucas was about 13 years younger than the seasoned detective.

Young punk. Hot Head. Voss missed him. Why couldn't that crazy arsonist have torched his little shack of a house. He took Lucas' family. His home. All of it, up in flames.

He took a swig from the bottle. He looked at the bible on his coffee table. 'Where were you on that one big man?' he thought to himself.

He took another swig of the bottle.

Voss was tired. Of everything. Of everyone. He needed to sleep but sleep would not come. Voss closed his eyes anyways.

At first he thought he managed to fall asleep finally. What threw him off was the silence. It wasn't the kind of silence that followed death or chaos. It was deliberate, expectant — a quiet that felt like the space between heartbeats.

The air itself shimmered with warmth, a sensation so foreign to him that he instinctively flexed his hands, expecting frost to bite. Instead, light coursed through him, tracing the lines of his muscles and bones, weaving him into something stronger, faster, more alive than he had ever been.

He rose from the cathedral floor, feeling every inch of his body as if it had been remade. His senses sharpened, the faint rustle of wings outside, the distant crackle of energy, even the subtle thrum of magic in the air. The world had a pulse now, and it beat in tandem with him.

What happened? Was this a dream? No, it wasn't. It was not a dream, this was really happening.

He looked down at his hands and the sigil. A golden feather. What was this?

He began looking around at the cathedral and noticed the familiar setting. This was Father Cael's church. It had been a long time since he had seen the inside of this building.

"This world is on the edge," a voice said behind him.

He spun around, hand instinctively going to the weapon at his side — but there was no threat. The figure that approached radiated calm authority. White robes flowed over the shoulders.

It was Father Cael.

"What is going on?" asked Voss "Why am I here?"

"I'm sure you have felt the presence that is not natural to this world detective." Said the priest in a calm tone.

Voss knew immediately what the priest was talking about. Lucas Cain. The Harrow. Voss nodded in acknowledgement.

"The Devil has found his warrior to destroy the barrier between our world and his. And now We have ours." The priest paused for a second "I received a message from the man upstairs" the priest motioned toward the sky.

"The message was simple and clear." Cael paused "We need to act. We have our feathered hand of Heaven. He is ready. Andre Voss."

"But why me? I'm done with this world." Stated Voss.

"Yes, yes you are done with this world Detective. You belong to the warmth of God and have been marked. The feather on your hand carries no weight. It carries the warmth of the Lord. You are the Hand of Heaven." Cael gave Voss time to process this new information.

"I can't fight Lucas. He is not the man we buried in St. Andrew's. He is a demon now. I saw the grave and the frost surrounding it." Voss stated.

Suddenly Voss felt a pain shoot through his body bringing him to his knees. What is this? What is happening to him he thought.

Then he felt them. Clawing their way out of his back. Voss opened his eyes to the sight of wings protruding from his back. They were elegant and radiated warmth.

"Flight," Cael said simply. "Reach beyond the earth. The light will carry you where you need to go, faster than any wings of bone could carry a mortal."

Father Cael stepped forward, placing a hand on Voss's shoulder.

"I know Lu was a like a brother to you. But that also puts you in a spot to bring him down or make him doubt his mission. Divide his followers. Melt the encroaching frost. Use the weapons of warmth to put things back the way they were and close this breach of Hell." Father Cael gestured, and a golden energy rose from the ground, coiling around Voss's arms, hands, and chest.

"You will need to learn quickly," Cael said. "The light will protect you from frostbite, from disease, even from mortal wounds, but you will not be invincible. Your judgment, your courage, your choices, these are the true weapons."

Voss flexed his hands. Golden strands of energy snaked along his veins, solidifying into forms he could manipulate. He could feel it responding to thought, to intent, like a living extension of his will.

Voss knew he had to stop The Harrow. At all costs. He gave the priest a nod of confirmation solidifying he knew what to do and turned towards the doors of the cathedral.

He stood for a moment, and he could tell that a good amount of time had passed since he fell asleep. A newspaper floating on the breeze caught his legs. Voss grabbed the paper and read the date.

October 2nd, 2025

He had fallen asleep in July. What has the Harrow accomplished in 3 months? Is his brother in arms too far gone at this point? He would find out, and he needed to do it fast.

"I guess it's time to put these wings to the test." Voss breathed to himself.

Voss leapt. For a heartbeat, the ground fell away, and then he was airborne. The city shrank below, streets twisting like veins of frost and ash. He felt exhilaration, but it was tempered by understanding, the next time he landed, it would be on a battlefield.

The Hand of Heaven has been dealt. Warmth was his weapon. Frost was his enemy.

Chapter Ten: The Hand and the Harrow

The city lay in ruin, frozen rivers of ash and frost carving jagged paths through streets that had once been familiar. Buildings leaned at impossible angles, glass shattered and glinting like ice shards. The scent of death lingered in the air, sharp and metallic, and the wind carried it across the skyline.

Voss hovered atop a crumbling rooftop, wings of golden light unfurling from his back. The warmth that coursed through him pulsed like a living heart, guiding him, tethering him to purpose. He could see the faint shimmer of the breach in the distance, pulsing sickly green through the clouds like a wound in the sky, a constant reminder of Lucas Cain's growing influence.

Father Cael's voice echoed in his mind, a steady guide:

"Follow the fractures. Where chaos gathers, the Harrow's influence will flow. The Wireborn cells are scattered, but they will converge where he tests their loyalty. Find them, disrupt them, and weaken the breach's grip on this world."

Voss adjusted his course, descending toward a district that had once been a bustling market. Now, it was a labyrinth of frost-choked alleyways and skeletal remains of stalls. He sensed movement, faint shifts of energy, life, and frost intertwining.

A small group of Wireborn scavengers moved in the shadows below. Their bodies were thin, pale, wrapped in scavenged armor, eyes glowing faintly with the frost that had marked them. They were young, inexperienced, and dangerous. But they were nothing compared to Lucas.

Voss landed silently behind a wall of shattered stone. His wings retracted, golden light dimming into the faintest shimmer. Razor-edged strands of energy coiled along his arms, ready to extend at his will.

The Wireborn scavengers had no chance to react before Voss struck. Golden strands erupted from his arms, lashing, grappling, and binding them in midair. Each movement precise, lethal, yet controlled, a demonstration of his newfound power without unnecessary cruelty.

Voss crouched beside the captured Wireborn, the faint warmth of his presence seeping into the frost that coated their skin.

"Who leads you?" he asked.

A young girl, barely older than seventeen, lifted her frostbitten face. Her voice was hesitant, trembling:

"We... we follow him. The Harrow. He... he promised a way out, promised us power... he promised freedom from the frost."

Voss's jaw tightened. Freedom, power, all the same lies that had corrupted so many. He could feel the pulse of the breach responding to her fear, to her loyalty, to the ripple of energy flowing from Lucas Cain himself.

"And you believe him?" Voss asked softly, golden light coiling along his arms.

She nodded, shivering.

"He said he would make the world ours. He said he would end the frost's bite... if we serve him."

Voss's wings unfurled slightly, a subtle reminder of what had been returned to him.

"He serves no one," he said. "Not the frost. Not the world. He serves only the breach, and it will consume him as easily as it consumes you if you continue down this path."

The girl's eyes flickered with doubt. It was small, barely perceptible, but it was there. A crack in the ice.

One of the Wireborn tried to strike back, a twisted spear of bone and wire, but Voss intercepted it mid-swing, bending it into a knot of light before it could harm him.

"Yield," Voss commanded, his voice steady and carrying the authority of his resurrection.

The Wireborn froze, wide-eyed. In the past, fear alone would have been enough for them to attack or flee. Now, they sensed something different, not malice, but inevitability. The light was stronger than frost, stronger than wire, stronger than the chaos Lucas Cain had spread.

Above them, the sky shimmered. The breach pulsed in sickly green, faint tendrils of frost and shadow weaving into the city below. Voss could feel its pull, the whisper of chaos calling him, challenging him, tempting him to act rashly.

But he did not. He steadied himself, letting the light guide his thoughts, letting judgment rule over instinct.

He had been returned for this purpose, not to strike blindly, but to shape the battlefield, to turn the tide, to weaken Lucas Cain's influence before the Harrow could consolidate power.

As Voss prepared to relocate his prisoners to a safer position, a shadow passed above. He looked up just in time to see Lucas Cain slicing through the skyline, wings of bone and rusted metal spanning wide, the air around him fracturing with frost.

Voss felt a chill that was not fear, it was recognition. He understood that this mission, this first engagement, was only the beginning. Lucas Cain was testing his reach, probing the defenses of both Wireborn and light-aligned warriors.

And somewhere in that sickly shimmer of green, the breach throbbed, hungry for the chaos it would draw from every act of violence, every fracture of loyalty, every moment of fear.

Voss released the captured Wireborn into a safe perimeter, watching as doubt and confusion began to creep into their minds. Some would escape, some would falter in loyalty, and some would eventually seek redemption. But each step, each choice, each moment was now part of the war.

"Nice to see you again brother." Lucas jested "been a while hasn't it?"

Voss stood and remained silent. Fists clenched.

"Nothing to say to your old partner? No jokes? Hmm tough crowd" Lucas let out a laugh that sent chills down Voss' spine.

"Lucas you have to stop this." Said Voss.

"Oh get out of here with that shit. You don't have to do this, you're a good man, what would your family think of what you have become?" Lucas said in a mocking tone.

"Come on Dre we've all seen the movies, and we know the lines. We're not doing that brother. Not today. Not ever." Lucas stated with conviction. "You will fall by my hand or join me. Those are the options. The frost accepts all. The wire binds all. I am inevitable."

Detective Voss acted without hesitation, testing his new weapons of light and warmth. Lucas blocked his attacks seemingly without any effort. Voss continued his assault trying to find an opening.

Lucas laughed as his former partner attacked him. He could tell this power was new to Voss so he was testing to see what he could do.

The sounds of something metal-on-metal clashing filled the air around them. Each attack seemingly hitting harder than the last.

Voss started growing concerned. Had it been too long already? The attacks continued.

"What's the matter Mr. 'Warrior of light'" Lucas jested making air quotes.

Voss stopped his assault. He could feel the use of his weapons draining him while Lucas shrugged off his assault as if Voss was a bothersome fly.

"This is futile Dre." Lucas stated.

"I must try Lu" Voss responded with doubt in his voice.

"Find me when you're ready to truly lose this battle. Or join me in this conquest. Choice is yours Dre." The Harrow hadn't given him time to even respond before he took to the sky in flurry of Frost and metal.

Voss felt the first hint of defeat.

This did not sit well with him.

Voss jumped into the air and spread his wings.

The city below showing significant signs of the frost taking over.

The frost had spread unnervingly fast.

The Hand.

The Harrow.

The warmth.

The frost.

Voss felt that the city he had called home his entire life was going to be consumed by this battle of warmth and frost. Thoughts of defeat raced through his mind.

He had to see this through to the end.

The sigil on his hand pulsed with warmth.

Chapter Eleven: The City of Frost

The city lay in ruin, frozen rivers of ash and frost carving jagged paths through streets that had once been familiar. Buildings leaned at impossible angles, glass shattered and glinting like ice shards. The scent of death lingered in the air, sharp and metallic, and the wind carried it across the skyline.

It was now approaching one year since The Harrow started his work. His cult had since become an army. Some of them broke off into their own Factions believing their own interpretation of the past year's events were 'true to the frost.'

It was all bullshit only Father Aurek had all the answers these lost souls were looking for. Everybody has their own ideas and opinions. Everybody sees things differently.

Idiots. But not useless, The Harrow's goal was chaos. Total chaos. Spread the frost like a plague.

Father Aurek understood why The Harrow didn't mind this happening. The more fractures, the faster the breach would open. They were each progressing things even faster than Lucas Cain anticipated.

Progress.

The Harrow's thoughts turned to the nearby city of Frosthaven. The name seemed to call to him. Everybody that survived the initial cleanse of the city of Archcrest fled to Frosthaven. Thinking themselves safe.

The city of Frosthaven had once been a hub of commerce and light. Now it had been

Boarded up in anticipation of the encroaching frost that had taken Archcrest. The only thing separating the two was the patch of land that housed St. Andrews Cemetery.

Coincidentally, St. Andrews Cemetery was established on that barren land because the land could not produce life. No matter how hard they tried in the beginning.

Seeing Frosthaven boarded up and guarding their warmth gave The Harrow a sense of power.

Look at you all. Cowering before the frost and wires.

Lucas turned toward St. Andrews Cemetery and gazed at the Breach. Pulsing. Breathing.

The city of Frosthaven will fall. The Harrow would give them hope. Then Destroy it. He sensed Voss was over there. Planning. Learning his power and becoming a danger to The Harrow. He has had his time.

He carried the warmth. He carried the hope. But the frost will consume all of it.

Patiently he waited.

Watching the city from the sky and feeling the panic within.

The Harrow was pleased.

Chapter Twelve: The Visit Within

The slaughterhouse stank of rot and cold metal.

Lucas sat on an overturned crate in the center of the frost-haloed floor, wings folded loosely behind him. Skeletal frames of bone, bristling with rusted metal feathers that caught the dim light like dying embers. Each movement made them creak, a sound halfway between brittle ice cracking and an old door groaning on its hinges.

Father Aurek and the Wireborn had not moved since kneeling. The youngest among them shivered from more than just cold; their eyes fixed on Lucas as though he were a living altar.

The Devil's voice had been silent since dawn. Now, it uncoiled inside Lucas's skull like smoke rising from embers.

"They are yours, Lucas. Their breath, their blood, their worship — all yours. Take them."

Lucas lifted his head, a half-smile touching his lips.

"I don't need your honeyed lies," he murmured under his breath.

Aurek's head tilted slightly, as though he'd heard, though he knew the words were not meant for him.

"Lies?" the Devil's voice rumbled, the tone mockingly wounded.

"Come on," Lucas said, standing slowly. The sound of metal grinding against bone whispered through the hall as his wings stretched, skeletal frames scraping frost from the hanging chains.

"I've known since you dug me out of the dark. You didn't have to promise me glory or vengeance. You didn't have to convince me I was chosen. I *want* this."

The frost spread from his feet in a visible wave, crawling up the walls, freezing old streaks of blood until they glittered.

"I'm not your reluctant weapon," Lucas continued. His voice echoed in the hollow space. "I'm not your pawn who thinks he's still pure. I'm all in. Every drop of warmth this world has left... I'll take it. I'll *help* you snuff it out."

Aurek lowered his head in reverence. The Wireborn pressed their bare palms harder into the ice, some whispering their frost-prayers.

"And why, Lucas?" the Devil's voice curled like black smoke in his thoughts. *"Why give yourself to me without chains?"*

Lucas looked toward the jagged holes in the roof, where pale light bled through the winter sky. "Because this world's been dying since long before you came knocking. I'm just cutting out the rot faster."

The Wireborn erupted into their hymns. The sound was a low and guttural chant that resonated through the slaughterhouse, voices layering over one another like grinding stones.

"Stillness to flesh, frost to blood... Bone to sky, rust to wing... Harrow, Harrow, make the world still..."

The air thickened with rime until every breath burned in the lungs. Lucas closed his eyes, letting the sound wash over him. For the first time since clawing out of the grave, he felt

not like a man dragged into darkness... but like
a king stepping into his throne room.

The Devil sat in the black chair, its back
curving like the ribs of some ancient beast. A
trophy.

His lair was not fire, nor molten stone but an
endless plain of ice and shadow. Where the
horizon vanished into a pale, source less light.
The air was so cold it stripped the moisture from
thought itself, leaving only clarity... and despair.

The Devil was dressed as always. An
immaculate black suit, crimson silk tie, cane
across his knees. His eyes glowed like hot coals
behind a mask of perfect calm.

He was looking into the window of the world
above. The chaos. The fractures within the
wireborn. All of them pieces to the puzzle.

He saw The Harrow hovering over Archcrest
planning his next move. Frosthaven. What a
fitting name for the next city to fall. The
wireborn shall take it with the guidance of their
Harrow.

The Devil smiled to himself on the thought.
Perfect.

Chapter Thirteen: Tragedy in Frosthaven

The city smelled of frost, metal, and decay. Archcrest had been taken, and the frost was quickly approaching. The Harrow had turned his sights on the last refuge of warmth and light. Frosthaven will fall. The Hand will fail to stop anything.

In the distance something was stirring within the walls of Frosthaven. The Harrow did not know of any Wireborn factions attacking ahead of schedule. Curious.

The Harrow leapt into the sky and spread his wings, and the sound of metal and bone filled the air near him. The trail of frost followed him like a loyal hound.

When he reached the walls of the city he could hear the battle raging within the walls of the city. He could see the faint traces of the frost. He could hear the faint singing of the hymns of the Wireborn.

This was something else. A fracture in the warmth. And the frost had seeped in. This was ahead of schedule. A divide amongst the 'righteous.' What could they be fighting about he wondered to himself. No matter the reason, it was still providing for the breach. Chaos is the key to open the door. Any form will do. The Harrow smiled as if he saw the victory ahead solidified.

Down in the city of Frosthaven there was a fierce battle raging in the streets. Andre Voss had been betrayed, and sides were chosen. Some believed the fight was futile. Some believed they had the strength to see this through to victory. Futility was right. And the divide amongst the Hand of Heaven's followers had now solidified that inevitability.

Father Cael had been a part of a recent pre-emptive strike to try and throw The Harrow off of his plan. During this clash Father Cael had been taken. The leader of this Wireborn faction had defeated him on the battlefield. The man was huge. Maybe a bodybuilder before the acceptance of the frost. His razor wire crown sitting askew on his head.

Jonathan Rowe had accepted the frost long ago after seeing the incident at the community center. He had worked at a store down the street and witnessed the altercation between the priest and the drunk man. Curiosity led him to investigate the confrontation. From a distance at least.

The drunk man made his way into the building toward the cafeteria where they were handing food out to the homeless with the priest, Father Aurek. Jonathan stepped into the building just in time for the man with wings and razor wire that seemed to come out of his arms to barge through the door. Jonathan was off to the side as the man that seemed to not belong to this world strode past him. Was he man? Or was he a monster? Jonathan was curious.

When the drunk man pulled out the gun and the gunshots filled the air, the beast of a man eliminated the distance between him and the gunman and in a split second the winged man had cut the man's hands off with the razor wire and wrapped him up like a snake finally catching its prey. The man seemed to explode in front of everybody in the cafeteria.

Jonathan cringed as the blood covered everyone, including himself. He knew then that he would follow this beast of a man wherever he would lead him to.

Father Cael opened his eyes, and the giant man stood before him.

"Mornin sunshine" said Jonathan mockingly to the tied-up priest. "Nice of you to finally join us Father"

"What happened?" inquired the priest, confused and his vision blurry.

"Your faith has betrayed you Father. I am going to show you something and you can either accept or be destroyed without question." Jonathan stated in a menacing tone.

The priest sat quiet. Contemplating the statement.

Jonathan Rowe turned to what seemed like a table made entirely of frost behind him and reached for something. When he turned back around he held a razor wire crown.

The priests' eyes widened with fear.

Father Cael thought of the fallen detective. Where was he? Why hasn't he come to save me? Why wasn't he on the battlefield with me? The Hand could've prevented this from happening. He remembered the last talk he had with the reborn detective. Father Cael had discussed the attack that could cripple the Wireborn and The Harrow.

The Hand said it wasn't time. Cael disagreed. He felt they were wasting their time just waiting for the frost to come instead of striking when

The Harrow least expected it. This had been when the divide started to form.

Father Cael had been wrong, for the Wireborn seemed to always be prepared for everything as if they saw into the future.

Cael looked at the razor wire crown in the giant man's hands. He felt the weight of defeat. It was over. The frost was inevitable.

"Do you accept the gift of the frost and wire?" Jonathan asked the defeated priest.

Cael thought on the question.

"Yes, I accept." The priest confirmed.

Father Cael had been initiated into the Wireborn. The hymns of the Wireborn filled the air.

The frost was inevitable indeed.

The Hand was alone. The Harrow was coming.

Chapter Fourteen: Preparation

Voss had been working on getting the hang of his powers for a long time now. The way Lucas Cain deflected his attacks as if they came from a small child had sowed the seed of doubt within him.

After his initial confrontation with The Harrow he knew he had to figure this power out and make it stronger. The more he used them the less he remembered about his life before becoming The Hand of Heaven.

He felt as though his humanity was leaving him, bit by bit. Eventually, he would be nothing more than an automaton. Taking direction without thought.

He had to try though. He had to try and save the warmth of Frosthaven. If Frosthaven were to fall, who knows where The Harrow may take this frost. How far could this spread? Would there be an end?

Most likely not he thought.

Three days ago he had figured out how to conjure weapons of pure warmth and light. He favored the axe of light he called it. It felt like the right tool to use. He had become good at throwing the axe and 'calling' it back to him without missing a step.

He had figured out how to use the wires of light more efficiently and accurately. The wings had their uses as well. Not just flight, but he could use them to grab and deflect as well.

But with every new thing he figured out, a memory slipped into the void.

Would good prevail over evil? Maybe, maybe not. He was determined to give his all in the final confrontation that loomed on the horizon. He didn't know when it would happen, but it would be soon he felt.

He had not heard from Father Cael since the argument. Cael thought it time to attack one of the main Wireborn factions led by a giant man by the name of Jonathan Rowe. Voss thought this a mistake to move before he was ready. Cael disagreed stating that Voss was taking too long and stormed off.

That was two days ago. Things were quiet apart from the warmth humming in the air from him manifesting new weapons and trying them out.

Then it happened. The pain shot through his hand. It felt cold and the feather sigil flickered as if it was a light not getting enough power.

At this moment he knew something had happened within his ranks as if he lost an important cog to his machine. The pain subsided and the sigil glowed bright again.

The time for preparation was over. He needed to act now.

Voss collected himself and started heading to the cathedral to speak with Father Cael about making their move. They need to save the warmth of the world. The frost cannot triumph. The Harrow must be defeated.

By any means necessary.

Chapter Fifteen: Inevitability

The Breach pulsed relentlessly a sickly green heartbeat feeding Lucas Cain's growing power.

Voss hovered high, wings heavy and golden strands flickering against the overwhelming pulse of the conduit. The battle had raged for hours, and every strike, every liberation, every attempt to disrupt the Harrow had been countered with brutal efficiency.

Lucas Cain perched atop the conduit, wings of bone and rusted metal unfurled like a dark cathedral. His presence radiated dominance, a palpable pressure that sent even the most defiant Wireborn into obedience.

"You fought bravely," he said, voice cutting through the freezing wind. "But the outcome was always inevitable. You cannot win against the Harrow."

Voss dove into the city, golden strands whipping across constructs, rescuing the few civilians who remained. His wings carried him like a storm, yet every movement felt heavier, slower, weighed down by the sheer power of the Harrow above.

He struck at nodes, shattered constructs, but Lucas Cain's countermeasures were instantaneous. Frost and wire erupted from every corner, forcing Voss into desperate defensive maneuvers.

I cannot stop him, Voss realized, eyes narrowing.

"You think you can challenge me?" Lucas hissed.

"The Breach is mine. The world is mine. Resistance is a fleeting illusion."

Voss countered The Harrow's sneak attack, golden strands wrapping around bone and wire, striking with all his strength. They collided in a storm of light and frost, golden feathers shredded against rusted metal, sparks flying from every point of contact.

With a surge of the conduit, the Breach pulsed violently, amplifying Lucas Cain's strength beyond mortal limits. Voss's strikes faltered, strands snapping, wings battered. The civilians below screamed as frost constructs surged forward, capturing any who remained defiant.

These were new tricks The Harrow had learned during the calm before the storm.

Lucas Cain struck with precision, bone and wire piercing defenses, severing golden strands, and forcing Voss back. Every node Voss disrupted was rapidly restored by the Harrow's power.

"You cannot defy me!" Lucas Cain roared. "I am inevitable. I am the Harrow. And now, the worlds are mine!"

Voss fell back, battered, exhausted, but still alive. The conduit's pulse stabilized, the Breach solidified, and the merged realms writhed under Lucas Cain's command.

The Breach had begun to fully open and sickly cold from Hell was seeping through at an alarming rate since Father Cael had defected and become Wireborn. The warmth fractured further escalating the progress of the breach.

Father Cael now led a group of defectors that were following Voss and his warmth.

The Harrow saw Voss' confidence falter. He was almost at his breaking point. The Harrow was on the brink of victory.

Voss collected himself and took in the scene below for a second. The battlefield below was chaotic and uncontrollable. He knew he had been defeated before the fight even ended. But he must continue, he can't let the world become a frosted wasteland.

There has to be something he can do. Voss' eyes fixed back on Lucas Cain. His wings keeping him in the air with the sound of creaking rusted metal and bone scraping together. Voss lunged forward wielding his axe of light and unleashed a desperate flurry of attacks.

The Harrow warded off the desperate attacks with little effort. His opponent had become tired. Voss continued the assault despite it being fruitless. The harrow let his guard down for a split second and Voss hit his flesh for the first time.

A small ray of hope.

The Harrow looked at his chest where the axe of light struck him. The wound already healing itself.

"Good one Voss." The Harrow taunted "too bad it's not enough. Your faith is faltering, and I can taste the desperation in your attacks."

"I am going to fight you until the warmth leaves my body." Voss growled back at him.

This time The Harrow made the first move.
Razor wire and gold light strands were sparking
and clashing around them. The Harrow and
The Hand were locked in a battle to the finish.
Each strike from the Hand of Heaven more
desperate than the last.

The Harrow dodged a blow from the axe of
light and with a swiftness that only The Harrow
could muster the battle ended. The Harrow's
razor wire had found its target.

"Goodbye brother. Your part in this has run
its course. You lost. I never hated you through
all this Voss." Said The Harrow in a somber
tone.

Voss let out his last breath and burst into a
fine golden dust that slowly drifted to the
ground. The battle that had been raging below
them stopped to take in the sight.

Only The Harrow remained in the sky
above.

After a brief pause to take in the fall of the
Hand of Heaven. As the fine golden dust settled
on the ground and was eaten up by the frost that
waited. The battle resumed and after a while the
sounds died out until all that was left were the
Wireborn.

The frost had taken hold, and the Breach
had opened.

The Harrow took in the sight of the fleeing
warriors that remained of Voss' forces.
Scattering. They were defeated. All hope was
lost for the warriors of the warmth and only the
frost remained.

The Hand.

The Harrow.

We are all Wireborn in the end.

The Devil was pleased with his Harrow.

But somewhere in a forgotten place surrounded by salty waters. Something stirred.

And then there was the Dark forest that was beyond his sight. The Devil did not care for these places of the world that were out of his sight through his window to the world above.

What is this? Why can't I see this forgotten place? Or this dark forest. This concerned the well-dressed man with the cane. He started pacing.

This must be investigated. The Harrow will see to it.

Chapter Sixteen: The World Notices

Bradley had just gotten home after a long day at the plant. Most days after work he turned to the news and drank his way to sleep. So far, today wasn't any different.

He took a swig of his freshly opened bottle and sat down in his comfy chair. After grabbing the remote and turning the TV on his day changed.

When the TV came on he was immediately bombarded with the events of Archcrest and Frosthaven. From the helicopter view it looked like they were focused on the world's largest snow globe.

Where the two cities should've been, was a warzone covered in frost. Frosthaven had fallen and the warmth fell with it. All that remained were the wireborn and The Harrow. And frost.

As the helicopter circled the area the newscaster described the Breach pulsating into the sky above.

His body tensed up at the sight that was on his TV. There is no way this was real, he thought.

The air above St. Andrew's cemetery pulsed, like a heartbeat. The thought sent chills down his spine.

"..... It appears as though the two major cities that were once a major hub for trade and commerce have befallen an unnatural winter storm. The storm seems to have been blocking communications in and out of the two cities for some time now. We have no word from inside the city....." announced the man on the TV.

Bradley took a long sip from his bottle and picked up his phone. His brother Mike lived in Archcrest.

No answer.

He dialed again. And again. And again. Nothing.

Bradley hadn't spoken to his brother in at least a couple years due to a falling out over a misunderstanding. After that, Mike moved to Archcrest, and they haven't spoken since.

Bradley had to go check on him.

As he started gathering his things to make the 4-hour trip to Archcrest something on the TV caught his attention.

At first the news broadcast went silent with an ominous tone as if the broadcast were terminated by the weather or something along those lines. The screen flickered.

Then a man appeared on the screen. He was well dressed in a three-piece suit, and he rested his hands on the top of his cane. There was nothing around him, only darkness that looked cold and uninviting.

The man seemed to smile at Bradley. Then he spoke in a voice as smooth as velvet.

"Good evening my scattered audience. Forgive the intrusion but you regularly scheduled illusions of safety must make room for truth." He paused.

"You've already heard whispers haven't you? Archcrest lies gutted, it's towers broken, and its people crawling in ash. Frosthaven, the once proud and shining city, has melted into ruin. These cities did not fall because of storms, armies, or politics. They fell because I allowed them to. And what I allow, I can unleash." The well-dressed man's face now filled the screen.

He smiled, showing too many teeth to be natural.

"You thought your wars, your faiths, your crowns, and your clever machines mattered. How quaint. But now, every flag you've ever saluted will burn in the fire. And your prayers will fall victim to that same fire. The age of men is a story that is at its end. The Breach has been opened, and the frost of Hell will cover your world. The Harrow is coming for you all. And the frost of hell comes with him."

The broadcast cut to black. Static hums like distant laughter.

Bradley, and the rest of the world knew who that was. It was the Devil. And his time of frost and ruin has come.

The frost will eat this world and shuttle it to oblivion.

Epilogue: And a Bottle of Rum

The island had no name on any map. From the sky it was nothing more than a dark blot of stone and jungle in the blue sea, a place ships gave wide berth without knowing why. In the town where they started the journey the locals called it cursed, though none could say where the story began. Sailors at the port where they departed from in search of the lost island whispered of wrecks near its reefs, of storms that brewed only when sails drew close.

But for five friends with cameras and sponsorships, it was perfect.

The big boat shuddered as it scraped the reef, tossing the group into shallow surf. They laughed, splashing each other, their voices too loud, too alive for a place that had not heard laughter in centuries.

"Bro, this is sick," one of them grinned, phone held high as he recorded. "Untouched island, never been explored, not on Google Earth, not anywhere."

Behind him, the others dragged waterproof packs onto shore. A girl in neon sneakers posed against the jagged cliffs. Another lit a cigarette, already narrating to her camera about "uncharted waters" and "real-life pirate legends."

Their words carried across the sand, brash and careless.

The island listened.

They found it before dusk, a gaping mouth in the cliffside, carved faces screaming from its stone.

"Yo, look at that!" the leader shouted, panning his camera across the grotesque carvings. "This is like... straight-up horror movie vibes."

"I bet it's some cult shit," the smoker muttered, flicking ash into the sand. "Or cannibals. Or both."

"Pirates," another corrected, smirking. "Didn't you read the blog? Supposedly some Captain Red-whatever got buried here."

"Redgrave," the girl with neon sneakers said, rolling her eyes. "God, you guys don't research. He was some psycho who got mutinied for black magic or whatever. They say his crew nailed him up in the cave and left him."

The others howled with laughter.

"Okay, okay, that's it. We're going in. Exclusive content, people. *Viral.*"

The air was damp and heavy. Their phone lights pierced the dark in sharp beams, illuminating moss, barnacle clusters, and spirals carved deep into the walls. Their sneakers slapped wet stone, their voices echoing louder than they realized.

The girl with the camera stopped suddenly. "Guys... what's that?"

The pool lay ahead, black as oil, perfectly still. And above it, half-sunk into the wall, was the crucifixion.

Redgrave.

Rags clung to his body. Barnacles crusted his arms. Rusted nails split through his wrists and ankles. His head slumped forward, his mouth slack, one eye socket hollow — but the other glimmered faint in their light.

The group gasped.

"No way," the leader whispered. His grin spread wide. "This is it. This is *real.*"

He panned his camera over the body, narrating with nervous laughter. "Guys, we just found the lost tomb of Captain Redgrave, pirate king, necromancer, whatever you want to call him. Dude's right here, nailed to the freakin' wall."

At the pool's edge lay the book.

The cover stretched yellow and cracked, the binding blackened with salt. Strange symbols wriggled faintly across its skin. The camera lights caught on it, making it seem to glisten.

The neon girl bent down, lifting it with a wrinkle of disgust. "Oh my god, it's like—made of leather or something."

"That's human skin," the smoker muttered with a smirk.

"Shut up," she shot back, laughing.

The leader shoved his phone close, recording every angle. "Yo, read it! Read some of it for the channel!"

"Dude, I'm not..."

"Come on, it'll blow up. Hashtag 'cursed pirate.' Just one line. What's the worst that could happen?"

The neon girl giggled, flipping it open. The pages were damp, the ink a dark, dried rust. She squinted, frowning. "I don't... I don't know what this says. It's like Latin or something."

"Then just say it! Pretend!"

And laughing, without thought, she spoke the first line she could sound out.

The cave exhaled.

The pool rippled.

Their laughter faltered as the air grew heavy, pressing against their chests. The torches sputtered. The walls groaned. The nailed corpse above the pool lifted its ruined head.

One eye burned green.

"Holy shit..." the leader gasped, stepping back, his camera clattering to the stone.

Redgrave's jaw cracked open. Barnacles split. His voice, a tide rolling through centuries, thundered across the chamber:

"My chains are broken. My vessel returns. My tide rises."

The pool erupted, black water spraying upward, drenching them all. Hands shot from the surface, pale, barnacled, clawing. The drowned surged forth, jaws gaping, groans deafening.

The influencers screamed.

And from the pool itself, another figure rose beside Redgrave — smaller, barnacle-crusted, pale-eyed, clutching a phantom tome against his chest.

Toby Cray.

First mate.

Redgrave spread his arms wide, water cascading down his rotted form. His laughter cracked the stone, split the island, and rolled into the sea.

The neon girl dropped the book, stumbling back, her screams cutting through the roar. The drowned lunged.

And Redgrave, his glowing eye fixed on the horizon, whispered with a smile:

"The world will drown."

The cameras kept recording.

Part 3
Whispers of the Tide and Tome

Prologue: The Mutiny

The sea that night was black glass, broken only by the heaving breath of the storm. Lightning flared across the horizon, painting the waves bone-white and jagged. The men on deck worked with silent urgency, their eyes fixed not on the thunderclouds but on the figure who stood at the prow, arms raised as though he commanded the heavens themselves.

Captain Silas Redgrave.

He was a man carved out of cruelty and charisma, feared more than loved, but followed all the same. His coat hung heavily with seawater and blood, his beard matted with salt. Around his neck rattled strings of teeth, rings stolen from corpses, bones of sailors long drowned. In his hands he clutched a book — its binding the sickly yellow of human skin, its pages etched in blood so dark it gleamed black when wet.

The crew had seen their captain kill men. They had seen him burn villages. But what they saw that night was worse.

He had hauled the broken corpse of a cabin boy onto the deck, a boy lost to fever two nights before. Redgrave crouched over the body, his voice curling in languages none of the men knew. The lightning seemed to answer his words. The body convulsed. The boy's dead eyes snapped open, milky, and rolling, and his jaw clattered as though he was struggling to speak.

That was the moment the men broke.

The mutiny began not with a shout but with a whisper, steel drawn in shaking hands, a dozen men stepping forward as one. Redgrave lifted his head, eyes burning with that mad fire of a man who believed the world itself should bow to him.

"You think me mortal?" he spat, his voice like the storm itself. "You think chains or nails or knives will take me? I am the tide. I am the grave beneath it. Betray me, and I shall be the last breath in your lungs."

But they came all the same.

They fought him on the deck until the planks ran slick. Redgrave cut two men down before they swarmed him, ropes and blades binding his arms. He laughed as they beat him bloody. Laughed as they dragged him ashore, up the cliffs, and into the gullet of the mountain that loomed over their island refuge.

The cave swallowed them in darkness. The men carried torches, their firelight catching shapes carved into the stone, spirals, runes, faces of the drowned etched deep into the walls. They ignored them. Their boots echoed, and with each step, the cave smelled more of rot and brine, as though the sea itself lived in the rock.

At last they came to the chamber. The cavern was vast, its ceiling lost in shadow, its floor broken by a pool of water so black it reflected nothing. The air tasted of rust and old blood.

They nailed their captain to the wall above the pool. Rusted iron spikes hammered through wrist and ankle, splitting flesh and stone. Redgrave's laughter never broke, though blood poured down his arms and dripped into the water below. When one man struck the final nail through his chest, Redgrave smiled, teeth pink with blood.

"You've given me roots," he whispered. "Now I will never leave."

The men threw his book at his feet, the vile tome he had carried like a crown. Its cover glistened wetly in the torchlight, obscene and grinning. They left it there as mockery, a reminder of his failure.

But Redgrave's eyes, even as his head slumped forward, still burned.

"You'll not see the horizon again," he croaked. "None of you. This island is mine. Your bones will be my chains, and your blood will keep me fed. I curse you, my brothers. I curse this stone, this water, this sand. None who betray me will leave this place."

And then he fell silent. The torches sputtered.

The men fled, leaving him crucified in the dark.

Behind them, in the echoing hollow of the mountain, the black pool rippled as if something deep beneath had stirred.

Chapter One: The Boy

The boy's bare feet touched stone.

It was damp and uneven, slick with moss and salt. The air inside the cave was colder than outside, carrying the bite of iron and brine. He shivered, though no wind touched him. The only sound was the slow drip of water somewhere deep within, a patient rhythm like the ticking of a clock.

The moonlight faded behind him after only a few steps. Shadows swallowed his thin form until he could not see his own hands. He pressed forward anyway, one palm on the wall to guide him. His fingers brushed grooves cut into the rock, not cracks, not natural lines, but shapes.

He stopped.

When he leaned close, squinting, he saw that the carvings were faces. Dozens of them. Eyes wide, mouths open in silent screams, their features eroded but unmistakable. Some were so small they looked like children. Others stretched long and thin, distorted as if drowned. He tore his hand back, his breath shuddering in his throat.

"Do not fear them."

The voice slid through his skull like cold water. It did not sound like a man speaking aloud, but like words whispered from behind his eyes.

The boy spun, but there was no one in the passage. The pirates were all in their huts, snoring into their cups. No one had followed him.

Still, the voice was there. Patient. Measured.

"They are not your enemy."

The boy licked his lips, which had gone dry despite the wet air. "Who... who are you?" His voice was small, swallowed whole by the cave.

No answer came at first. Only the drip... drip... drip. Then the voice again, low as the tide retreating:

"One who was bound. One who waits."

The boy hugged himself, bones rattling beneath his skin. He thought of the stories Garrick had told — of the dead captain, of curses, of storms that kept men chained to the island. His fear pressed down like a heavy net. But another feeling stirred beneath it. Curiosity.

For the first time in his life, someone spoke to him without contempt.

He took another step forward. His eyes began to adjust to the dark, or else the dark itself shifted to let him see. The walls glistened with veins of salt. Strange barnacles clustered in patches, even here far above the sea. They pulsed faintly, as if alive.

The tunnel widened. He smelled something stronger now, the rank of rusted iron, mixed with the sour rot of stagnant water. Ahead, the sound of dripping grew louder, echoing from a chamber just out of sight.

"Closer."

The boy hesitated. His stomach twisted with hunger and fear. He thought of Blacktooth Vane's fist, the laughter of the crew, the endless lash of cruelty. Then he thought of the voice, deep and knowing, speaking to him as if he were not a rat, but a boy. A person.

He moved forward again.

The tunnel ended in a cavern. The ceiling vanished into shadow, but the chamber itself glowed faintly with phosphorescent lichen clinging to the rock. In the center of the floor stretched a pool of water so black it reflected nothing. No ripple touched its surface, though the air above it felt heavy, as though the water pulled at his breath.

On the far wall, he saw them.

Rust. Iron. Shapes that at first seemed like a tangle of seaweed. Then he saw the nails, long as daggers, hammered into stone. And the stains beneath them, dark, brown-black, feeding into the pool.

The boy's chest tightened. His knees nearly buckled. Every story whispered by the fire was true.

"There you are."

The voice came not from around him, but from above the pool, from the crucified shadow that hung half-sunken into the rock. The boy could not make out the face, not fully, but he saw the outline of a figure, slumped, and rotted, draped in rags that clung like seaweed. Barnacles spotted its arms. One eye socket glimmered faintly in the lichen glow.

The boy clapped a hand over his mouth, stifling a cry. His heart pounded, his body screamed to run, but his feet rooted to the stone.

The figure shifted. Only slightly. Just enough that the nails groaned in protest.

"You have been beaten. Mocked. Cast aside."

The boy's hand shook against his mouth. He did not answer.

"I know what it is to be cast aside."

The cavern seemed to breathe with the voice, each word pressing against his chest.

The boy's eyes darted toward the passage behind him. He should run. He should flee. But the thought of leaving, of returning to the fire, to fists and laughter at his expense, filled him with more dread than the corpse on the wall.

He lowered his hand. His whisper cracked with fear and longing.

"...what do you want from me?"

The shape above the pool smiled.

Chapter Two: Legends of the Dead Captain

Morning came with the stink of rum and rotting fish.

The boy sat on the sand, hugging his knees, staring out at the water. The surf broke gently against the beach, the waves carrying flecks of foam like pale scraps of cloth. To anyone watching, he looked like a child still half-asleep, wasting time before his chores began. But behind his hollow eyes burned the image of the figure in the cave, nailed against the stone, barnacles sprouting from his wounds, voice rising from the black water like the tide itself.

"You have been beaten. Mocked. Cast aside."

The words followed him into the dawn.

The men stirred one by one, coughing, groaning, cursing the brightness. A few sprawled where they had fallen the night before, sand clinging to their beards, flies buzzing at their lips. The boy quickly moved to his duties — fetching buckets of water, hauling driftwood for the cookfire, scraping crusted pans clean with a shell. The faster he worked, the less he was noticed.

But even in their hangovers, the pirates noticed his eyes.

"You look like you seen a ghost, rat," one of them jeered as he staggered past. He cuffed the boy across the head, knocking him into the sand. The others laughed, though it was not the same sharp laughter he knew so well. There was unease in it.

That unease grew later when the men gathered at the firepit. Old Garrick was there, his ruined nose whistling as he breathed. He had been the one to tell the story before, and the boy had thought perhaps it was only rum-madness. But now others pressed him for more, and the boy listened with hungry silence.

"Aye," Garrick croaked, his voice like wet rope dragged across stone. "I told ye, Redgrave was no man of flesh alone. He dealt in shadows, in voices, in things crawled up from the sea-bottom. The crew that nailed him thought they were free of him, but none of them ever saw home again. Not one."

"Storms wrecked 'em," muttered another pirate. He spat into the fire. "Ships split like toys. Masts turned to rot in a single night."

"Aye," Garrick said, nodding. "And when their bones washed ashore, the crabs wouldn't touch 'em. Nor the gulls. They lay there till the waves dragged them back to the pool."

The men shifted uneasily. Some made signs against evil. One man swore and stood, throwing his cup into the sand. "Enough of that!" he barked. "It ain't but stories. Ghost tales for children."

But the boy saw his hands shake when he reached for his knife.

That night, as the men drank deeper, the stories did not stop.

Around the firelight, their faces hollowed by shadow, they spoke of the caves.

Of men who had vanished near the mountain. Of strange lights that glimmered in the fog when the moon was gone. Of singing heard at dawn, the voices of women beneath the waves, though no woman had set foot on the island for years.

One man swore he had seen a figure standing at the mouth of the cave, arms outstretched, dripping black water. Another spat that it was only moonlight on stone. They argued, voices rising, until knives flashed and Garrick had to step between them with his pistol.

The boy said nothing. He only listened.

Every word they spoke matched what he had seen with his own eyes. The faces carved into stone. The barnacles clinging to the wall. The voice that slid through his mind like a tide filling a hollow shore.

When at last the men collapsed into sleep, the boy slipped away.

The jungle pressed close around him, its leaves sharp as blades, its insects whining in his ears. But he was not afraid. Not of the dark, not of the trees, not of the mountain that loomed above.

The fear he carried now was of something greater, not the cruelty of pirates or the sting of fists, but of what lay in the cave waiting for him.

He crept near the entrance, stopping short of the carved threshold. His breath shivered in his chest. The moon was low, its light slanting across the stone faces that ringed the cave mouth. Their eyes seemed to shift in the shadows, their mouths warping with each flicker of cloud.

The boy whispered into the dark.

"...are you still there?"

The cave answered.

"I am always here."

His heart leapt. His body wanted to flee, but his feet carried him forward. Just as they had the night before.

The same drip of water echoed. The same stench of brine and rust seeped into his nose. The same black pool stretched before him, bottomless, still.

And above it, still nailed to the stone, was the shape of the captain.

The boy dared a step closer than before. His bare toes reached the edge of the pool. The water lapped once, just once, though no ripple should have moved it.

The voice deepened, patient, rolling through his bones like the sea:

"They laugh at you. They strike you. They call you less than nothing. But you... you are not nothing. You are chosen."

The boy's eyes filled with tears. He thought of Vane's fists, of Garrick's laughter, of the endless jeers and names. He thought of how no one had ever called him anything but rat.

"Chosen?" he whispered, trembling.

The corpse on the wall stirred. Nails shrieked in the stone. Its head tilted, and the boy saw one eye glimmer faintly, like a pearl buried in rot.

"I will teach you their fear."

The pool rippled again, though the boy had not touched it.

He staggered back, heart pounding. And yet, though terror drenched his bones, he could not bring himself to leave.

By dawn, the boy had crept back to the camp, his body shaking, his eyes raw from sleeplessness.

The men were stirring, cursing at the pale light, already demanding rum. None looked at him twice. None saw how his hands trembled, how his lips moved in silence as though still speaking to someone who was not there.

No one but the mountain.

And the mountain whispered back.

Chapter Three: The Call of the Caves

The boy had not meant to linger so long.

He told himself he would only listen. Only stand at the edge of the pool until the voice soothed the ache in his chest, until he felt less like a beaten animal and more like someone who mattered.

But the cave always held him longer.

The whispers coiled around him like a tide that dragged and pulled, steady, patient, impossible to resist. His eyes traced the barnacle-crusted figure on the wall, his ears strained for every syllable that bled from the stone. Hours melted. Hunger vanished. Sleep no longer mattered. Only the voice.

"You are mine," it said. *"You are the first in a long age to step willingly into my shadow. That makes you more than they can ever be."*

The boy trembled with both pride and dread. He wanted to believe. He feared to believe. But the words pressed against the hollow places in him, and he felt filled for the first time in his life.

He did not hear the footsteps until it was too late.

"Rat."

The word cracked like a whip.

The boy spun, his blood turning to ice. A figure stood in the tunnel, framed in the pale lichen glow. Blacktooth Vane. His teeth glimmered white in his tattooed jaw, though the grin was one of cruelty, not amusement. His hand gripped the hilt of a curved cutlass.

"What's this?" Vane stepped closer, his boots crunching against damp stone. "Crawling off where no man dares go? Playing with shadows, eh? Maybe you've been stealing, hiding trinkets down here. Maybe you've been whispering to the bones."

The boy's throat locked. He wanted to speak, to lie, to explain, but no words came.

Vane's grin widened. He shoved the boy hard against the wall. "You stink of it. The curse. A rat sniffing round the grave of Redgrave himself." He spat on the ground, then raised his blade. "Best to cut your throat now, before you bring his rot into camp."

The boy whimpered, eyes wide, his back pressed to the damp stone. He could smell the rust on Vane's blade, see the flicker of madness in his eyes.

Then the cave answered.

The black pool rippled.

The sound was soft at first, like water stirred by a finger. But the ripples spread wider, faster, until the whole pool churned without wind, without touch.

Vane froze, his grin faltering. His eyes darted to the water. "What in—"

A hand shot from the pool.

It was not flesh but something pale and rotted, barnacle-crusted, dripping brine. Fingers like hooks wrapped around Vane's ankle.

The pirate howled, hacking down with his cutlass. The blade met water, but the grip did not loosen. Another hand burst forth, clawing at his calf, then another at his thigh. The pool foamed black as more hands clawed from its depths — the hands of the drowned, pale, and shriveled, veins filled with salt, nails cracked and sharp as shell.

They dragged him down.

Vane's scream tore the chamber. He slashed and kicked, his boots thudding against stone, but every movement only sank him deeper. The boy pressed against the wall, watching with eyes wide in horror.

"Help!" Vane shrieked at him. "Help me, rat!"

The boy could not move. Could not breathe.

The last thing he saw was Vane's tattooed jaw breaking the water, teeth still bared in a rictus grin before the black pool swallowed him whole. The surface stilled. Not a ripple remained.

The cave fell silent.

The boy's chest heaved. His pulse thundered in his ears.

Then the voice spoke again, calm, and cold.

"Do you see?"

The boy stared at the pool, tears trembling on his lashes. His voice came out in a whisper. "You... you killed him."

"He raised his hand against you. I do not suffer such men."

The boy shook his head, though his body trembled not with refusal but awe. "But he was strong. He was..."

"He was nothing." The word cracked like stone splitting. *"Steel and rum do not make a man strong. Strength is in will. In knowing who deserves breath and who deserves the water."*

The boy's legs gave out. He sank to his knees, staring at the still surface of the pool.

"You are chosen," the voice said again. *"They will fear you, as they once feared me."*

The boy clutched his head in his hands. For the first time, he did not feel only fear.

He felt power.

When he staggered back into camp hours later, his clothes damp, his skin pale, none of the pirates noticed his trembling. They were too busy drinking, too busy cursing Vane for wandering off into the jungle again.

The boy sat by the fire, silent, his eyes fixed on the mountain.

He did not tell them what he had seen. He did not need to. The mountain whispered for him.

Chapter Four: Punishment

The water swallowed him whole.

Vane's cutlass spun from his grip, tumbling into the void. His body thrashed, bubbles ripping from his throat as he kicked against hands that dragged him deeper, deeper still. Salt burned his eyes, but through the blur he saw them, faces. Dozens. Hundreds. Men with seaweed hair and barnacles bursting from their cheeks, mouths slack and spilling sand.

Their eyes glowed faintly, not with life, but with hunger.

No, Vane thought, his chest screaming for air. *I'm no weakling, I'm Blacktooth, I've gutted navy men, I've lived through shot and storm, no water's taking me—*

Another hand seized his throat. His vision darkened. He saw the boy's pale face at the edge of the pool, wide-eyed and still, watching him vanish.

The rat... the rat brought me here.

And then, as the sea stuffed itself into his lungs, his last thought was not of gold, nor women, nor victory, but of the iron nails he glimpsed in the shadows above, the crucified shape smiling as the blackness claimed him.

The boy woke screaming.

He had not remembered closing his eyes, but at dawn he found himself curled in the sand beside the firepit, breath ragged, chest aching as though he had drowned himself. The pirates stirred, casting him glares, but no one spoke.

Blacktooth Vane was gone.

The men grumbled as they drank their morning rum. Some claimed he had deserted. Others said he had staggered off into the jungle to sleep off a hangover. By noon, whispers began to shift. No man vanished alone on the island without cause.

"The mountain took him," Garrick muttered, his ruined nose wheezing with each word. "Mark me, the captain's curse is stirring again."

The boy kept his head bowed, saying nothing. He felt the truth burning inside him like fever, but to speak it would mean his own death. Or worse.

By nightfall, suspicion had sharpened.

"You," snarled Kellan, a broad brute with a scar splitting his lip, "you were seen skulking. Rat-boy, always slinking off when no one's watching." He seized the boy by the collar and hauled him into the firelight. "What'd you do, eh? Lead Vane into the dark?"

The boy shook his head, eyes wide. "No—no, I swear, I didn't..."

The back of Kellan's hand silenced him, blood springing at his lip. The men jeered, though their laughter was brittle, uneasy. The curse had touched them again, and laughter was the only shield they knew.

They bound the boy's wrists with rope and dragged him to the edge of the camp. "Let the tide decide," someone muttered. "If the sea spits him back, we'll know he's cursed."

They shoved him into the shallows, waves slapping cold against his face. He gasped, coughing saltwater, fighting against the bindings.

The men stood on shore, their silhouettes jagged in the firelight, waiting.

The tide crept higher.

The boy thought he saw movement in the deeper water. Pale shapes rising, barnacled hands just beneath the surface. Terror froze him. Was this punishment from the crew, or was it Redgrave calling to him again?

Then, just as his knees buckled beneath the weight of the tide, the rope slackened.

He blinked. The knots had come undone.

No pirate had moved to free him. They were still on shore, watching, muttering, restless. The boy felt the rope slide from his wrists as if unseen fingers had plucked it loose.

"No chain holds you while I watch."

The voice curled through his mind like smoke.

The boy stumbled from the surf, soaked, coughing. The pirates fell silent. They had expected him to drown or beg. Instead, he stood there, dripping and pale, his eyes wide but unbroken.

"Cursed," one man spat, backing away.

"Aye," muttered another, his voice shaking. "The captain's hand is on him."

The boy did not deny it. He could not.

Because in his chest, beneath the fear and salt, he felt something bloom. Not joy. Not pride. Something sharper.

Power.

That night, as the crew argued and drank in uneasy silence, the boy crept once more to the mouth of the cave. His body ached, his lip still bled, but his steps were steady.

The voice met him before he entered.

"You are stronger than they know. Stronger than they will ever be."

He pressed a trembling hand to the stone, where faces carved into the rock seemed to smile faintly in the moonlight.

"What do you want of me?" he whispered.

The cave exhaled. The pool within rippled, though he had not yet stepped inside.

"Only to give you what was taken from me. A crew. A legacy. An ocean that bends at your will. All you must do... is trust me."

The boy closed his eyes. For the first time, he did not feel like a rat.

He felt chosen.

Chapter Five: First Blood

The night was loud with thunder, but the storm never touched the island. Lightning flared beyond the horizon, a sea's length away, yet the air here was still, heavy, suffocating.

Toby Cray sat apart from the pirates, staring into the fire until his eyes burned. Every muscle ached from labor, every bruise on his thin body throbbed with memory. He could still taste saltwater from where they had tried to drown him the night before.

The men drank harder than usual. They argued over Vane's disappearance, voices sharp, laughter forced. Old Garrick muttered about curses until someone silenced him with a punch. Others swore Toby had led Vane astray, that he carried bad luck in his bones.

No one spoke his name. They never had.

Rat. Boy. Cursed.

But in the silence between the men's words, the mountain whispered another name.

"Toby."

He went to the cave after midnight.

The jungle was alive with insects and the hiss of leaves stirring in a breathless wind. The boy crept barefoot, every step familiar now, as if his body had begun to memorize the path. The carvings at the cave mouth no longer looked like warning — they looked like welcome.

The air swallowed him when he entered, damp and cool, rich with brine.

The pool was waiting. Always waiting. Above it hung the nailed figure of Redgrave, slumped but not dead, never dead. His voice came before his head lifted, a rasp in Toby's skull.

"You return to me."

Toby's lips trembled, but he nodded. "They, they hate me. They want me gone. You're the only one who..." His voice cracked. He bit his lip, hard enough to draw blood.

The figure's head shifted. The faint lichen glow caught on the glimmer of one eye.

"The only one who sees you."

"Yes." Toby's whisper spilled like a confession. "Yes."

At the pool's edge lay the book.

The tome was bound in something that should not have been skin, its surface yellow-gray and stretched taut like a drum. The edges curled with salt, as though it had once been drowned but never decayed. Symbols etched in rust and blood writhed faintly in the lichen light, their strokes too sharp, too alive.

The first night Toby had seen it, he had not dared touch it. But tonight, his fingers reached before his mind could stop him.

The cover was warm.

He pulled his hand back as though stung. His heart raced. But the warmth called him, and again his palm pressed against it, trembling. He imagined curling against it like a child with a blanket, imagined holding it tight so no hand could strike him, no voice could mock him.

"Is it... mine?" he whispered.

The voice that answered was not only in his head this time. The nailed corpse's mouth moved, the words crawling out like smoke.

"It has always been yours."

Toby clutched the tome to his chest.

For the first time in his life, he felt safe.

The whispers of the book filled his ears. They did not sound like words at first, more like waves crashing, or sails tearing, or bones breaking beneath the sea. But in those sounds was comfort. In those sounds was a promise: he was no longer alone.

He lay down at the pool's edge, the tome cradled against his ribs and closed his eyes.

And he dreamed.

He stood on a ship made of black wood, its masts shrouded in rags that dripped brine. The crew were shadows, eyeless, faceless, moving as one to the pull of the tide. At the helm stood Redgrave, not nailed to stone, not bound, but whole. His coat was ragged silk, his hat crowned with seaweed, his eyes two lanterns burning deep green.

"Captain," Toby whispered.

Redgrave's hand fell heavy on his shoulder, strong and cold. "My Toby."

The shadow crew bowed their heads at once, as though the boy were kin to their master. Toby's heart swelled. For once, no one called him rat. No one laughed.

The sea stretched endless and black, waiting for them.

"You will sail with me," Redgrave murmured, his voice the tide itself. *"Together, we will drown the world."*

Toby smiled in his dream, clutching the tome close.

When dawn came, the boy woke in the cave with the book still pressed to his chest. He did not want to let it go. He carried it beneath his shirt as he staggered back to camp, eyes heavy, mouth dry with salt.

The men noticed.

"Oi, rat," snarled Kellan, grabbing him by the arm. "What's that you're hiding?" He shook Toby hard, his fist raised.

The boy clutched the tome tighter. "N-nothing..."

The other men drew closer, suspicion bright in their bloodshot eyes. Garrick's ruined nose whistled as he leaned forward. "He's got the captain's stink on him. I told ye. The curse marks him."

"Best slit his throat," someone muttered.

The boy's breath came fast. His arms curled protectively over the book, trembling. He wanted to beg, to scream, but another voice drowned out his fear.

"Do not yield."

It rose from the tome itself, deeper than any whisper before.

"They cannot touch what is yours."

The men closed in, their hands rough, their blades glinting. But the air shifted. The fire at the center of the camp sputtered, flared high, then died as though snuffed by unseen hands.

The pirates froze.

From the direction of the mountain came a sound, low, dragging, like chains pulled across stone. The air grew damp, heavy with salt.

The men stepped back, muttering curses, making signs against evil. No one dared seize the boy again.

Toby clutched the tome tighter, his heart thundering. He had not spoken, had not moved — but Redgrave had answered for him.

For the first time, the pirates looked at him not as prey, but with fear.

That night, Toby sat apart again, the tome pressed against his chest like a shield. The pirates avoided him, whispering into their cups. He did not care.

Because in the cave, in the book, in the whispers, he had found something greater than all of them.

A captain. A master.

A safe place in the arms of the dead.

Chapter Six: Ghosts of the Drowned

The wind carried voices that night.

Not the rough, slurred songs of pirates in their cups, nor the hiss of insects in the trees, but something older. Something colder.

Toby Cray sat alone on the sand with the tome pressed against his chest, listening to the surf. At first, the sound of waves was steady, familiar, harmless. But slowly, beneath the hiss and crash, came another rhythm. Words carried on the tide. A chant in no tongue he knew, rising and falling with the pulse of the sea.

The hairs on his arms stood stiff. He hugged the tome tighter.

From the corner of his eye, he saw them.

Shapes at the shoreline.

Not men, not shadows, but pale things half-buried in the surf. Their hair streamed with seaweed. Their mouths gaped open, spilling sand and brine. Their hands twitched, clawing the beach as if they crawled upward from the sea itself.

The drowned.

Toby's breath hitched. He wanted to run, but his legs felt locked. The shapes shuddered once, twice, then collapsed into the foam and were gone, as if the tide had never carried them at all.

The boy swallowed, throat dry. He did not scream. He did not even whimper. Because some part of him knew they had not come to harm him.

They had come because of him.

The crew was not so calm.

By morning, the camp boiled with argument. Two men had vanished overnight — their boots found at the water's edge, but no bodies, no blood, only wet sand, and gulls circling above the waves.

"It's the boy," snarled Kellan, his scarred lip twitching. He jabbed a filthy finger toward Toby, who crouched at the edge of the camp, scraping barnacles from a pan. "Ever since he started sniffing round the mountain, men've been disappearing. Vane, now these two. He's marked."

"Cursed," Garrick agreed, his ruined nose whistling. "I told ye, the dead captain's hand is on him."

Toby kept his eyes down, pretending not to hear, though every word hammered into his skull. His fingers clutched the tome hidden beneath his ragged shirt. He wanted to protest, to shout that he was not their enemy, but another voice whispered against his thoughts.

"Do not defend yourself. They are not worth your breath."

That evening, as the sky bruised purple with twilight, three pirates cornered him.

Kellan led them, scar splitting his grin, a knife in his hand. Behind him stood Garrick and a wiry man named Holt, whose eyes were yellowed with sickness but sharp as a hawk's.

"Where've ye been skulkin,' rat?" Kellan growled, pressing Toby against the wall of a half-rotted hut. "What'd ye bring back with ye from the cave? Ghosts? Storms? Death itself?"

"I didn't..." Toby tried, but the knife bit against his throat, silencing him.

"You stink of him," Garrick spat, face so close the boy smelled rot in his breath. "Redgrave. His curse is on you. Best to cut it out before it spreads."

Holt's hand darted, seizing at Toby's shirt. He ripped it open, and there it was, pressed against Toby's chest, the book.

The pirates froze.

The lichen-stained skin cover glistened faintly in the torchlight, its symbols writhing as if alive. A pulse of warmth bled from it, and Toby felt it thrum against his ribs like a heartbeat.

"The captain's tome," Garrick rasped, his voice breaking. "He carries the captain's very book."

Kellan's knife pressed harder. "Then we end him now, before he ends us."

The pool stirred.

Toby had not left the camp. He had not stepped into the mountain's cave. And yet, in that instant, he felt it, the black water moving, the chains on the nailed figure groaning, the captain's voice flooding his head.

"Hold it tight, Toby. Do not fear. You are my vessel. Through you, I will breathe again."

The air thickened. The torches guttered. Salt burned the pirates' throats. From the shadows of the huts came a sound like wet footsteps, dragging, shambling closer.

The men spun, knives drawn, eyes wide.

No one was there. Yet the sound echoed. Louder. Closer.

Holt swore, dropping his torch. "The drowned..."

The fire hissed out in the sand. The night swallowed them whole.

Toby did not move. He clutched the book as if it were his own skin. Kellan's knife wavered. Garrick muttered prayers through his ruined nose. And then, just as suddenly, the air eased. The sound of footsteps faded.

Silence.

The pirates backed away, pale as bone.

"This ain't natural," Kellan spat, though his voice shook. He pointed his knife once more at Toby. "You keep your distance, rat. Or I'll gut you, curse, or no curse."

They fled into the night, their bravado hollow, their fear souring the air.

Toby slid down the hut wall, breath shuddering, the book still pressed to his chest. He wanted to cry, but the tears would not come. Instead, he felt a strange calm, heavy and cold, like the weight of the tide.

He had not been alone. He would never be alone again.

Deep in the mountain, nailed to stone, the corpse of Captain Silas Redgrave stirred.

His head hung forward, his flesh sagging with centuries of rot, but his mind was sharp as broken glass. He had watched through the boy's eyes, felt through the boy's trembling hands.

The crew's fear fed him. The boy's devotion sustained him. And the book, his book, pulsed in living flesh once more.

Soon.

"Little Toby," Redgrave whispered, though no one was near to hear. His words echoed in the chamber, rippling across the black pool.

"You clutch my heart to your chest as if it were your own. Through you, I will unmake my chains. Through you, I will drink the world again."

His nailed wrists groaned. Rust flaked from the spikes.

The tide inside the mountain shifted, and Redgrave smiled with what lips he still had.

"All vessels break. But before you shatter, boy, you will carry me past the reef. You will carry me home."

Chapter Seven: The Pact

Toby Cray sat at the pool's edge, the tome in his lap. The black water reflected nothing, yet he felt it watching him. It breathed with him, slow and patient, pulling his thoughts deeper into its silence.

He had not eaten in a day. His belly gnawed at him, but the hunger meant nothing. The jeers of the pirates, the sting of their fists, even the fear of death, all of it was distant now, softened by the steady voice that filled his mind.

"You are ready."

Toby lifted his head. Redgrave's rotted form still hung nailed to the cavern wall, but his presence filled the chamber like a tide filling a hollow shore. One eye glowed faint in the gloom, and the lichen shimmered green on the barnacles sprouting from his ribs.

"What do you want from me?" Toby whispered. His voice cracked. He was not a man, not even close, but he spoke as though bargaining were possible.

"Not want. Need." The captain's voice rasped like waves through broken timbers. *"I need your hands where mine are bound. I need your voice where mine is silenced. You will be the vessel of my will, and through you my chains will break."*

Toby clutched the tome tighter. "And what do I get?"

The captain's mouth cracked open, the sound a wet tearing. A smile, jagged, ruinous.

"Power."

The word alone carried weight. Toby felt it in his bones, in his teeth, in the bruises of every blow the pirates had ever laid on him. Power. Enough to stand taller than their laughter. Enough to end their fists. Enough to never be a rat again.

He stared at the pool, his reflection absent in the blackness. "I don't want to be afraid anymore."

The captain's voice softened, coaxing, fatherly and cruel all at once.

"Then place your hand upon the water."

Toby hesitated, heart hammering. He thought of Vane, dragged screaming below. He thought of Garrick's whispers, Holt's yellow eyes, Kellan's knife. He thought of his life, small and beaten, and the promise that he might be more.

He reached out.

His fingers brushed the pool. Cold surged through him, salt burning his veins, but he did not pull away. The water rippled beneath his touch, glowing faintly where his skin pressed it.

"Done," Redgrave breathed.

The pool stilled. The cave grew quiet again.

But Toby felt it, something inside him shift. His skin prickled, his heart heavy with an unfamiliar rhythm. It was as if the tide itself had taken residence in his chest.

He was not alone anymore. He would never be alone again.

The pirates knew something was wrong before dawn.

Their fire smoldered low, their rum tasted of brine, and the gulls screamed endlessly overhead. Unease clung to the camp like fog.

Kellan muttered that they should kill the boy and be done with it. Garrick whispered that it was already too late. Holt sharpened his blade with nervous hands.

Then came the scream.

It tore from the tree line at the edge of camp. The men rushed, knives and pistols ready, but what they found rooted them in silence.

A body lay sprawled across the sand, bloated, white, its flesh waterlogged. Its eyes were empty sockets, its skin covered in barnacles. What scraps of tattooed ink remained on the jaw made it plain.

Blacktooth Vane.

Kellan swore and staggered back. "He was, he was just..."

But Vane's corpse did not look days dead. It looked years dead. Decades.

Before anyone could speak, Garrick let out a strangled cry. He pointed with a trembling, ruined hand.

Three more bodies lay further up the shore. Holt's thin frame, already collapsing inward. Kellan's broad chest split open, crawling with crabs. Garrick himself stared into his own face — lips blue, skin sagging, the hole where his nose had been filled now with seaweed.

They stood, alive, breathing, blades in hand. And yet their bodies lay before them, rotten, decayed, drowned long before this night.

The boy stepped from the trees, the tome clutched to his chest. His eyes were wide but no longer pleading. The men turned toward him with terror, not rage.

"What trick is this?" Holt snarled, though his voice shook. He gestured at the corpses. "Some devilry, boy. Some—some curse you've loosed!"

Toby said nothing. His silence was answer enough.

Because behind his ribs, beneath his skin, the captain's laughter filled him, low and patient, curling in his marrow like smoke.

Deep in the mountain, nailed to the wall above the black pool, Silas Redgrave's head lifted. His rotted smile split wider as the tide lapped higher at his feet.

He had shown them a glimpse, nothing more than a sliver of his true reach. But it was enough. Fear was stronger than steel, and now it seeped into every corner of the camp.

"Yes," he whispered, watching through Toby's eyes, feeling through Toby's trembling hands. *"Fear them, boy. Feed on it, as I do. Every cry, every shudder, every heartbeat that flees — all of it will be ours."*

The nails groaned in the stone. Flakes of rust pattered into the pool below.

"Soon."

The drowned stirred. The pool whispered. And Redgrave dreamed of freedom.

Chapter Eight: The Drowning

The camp did not sleep.

After the discovery on the shore, no man dared close his eyes. The bodies had been dragged into the shallows, but the tide refused to carry them away. They lay where the waves could not quite claim them, bloated and barnacled, their skin flaking like wet parchment. The gulls wheeled above but would not descend. Even the crabs scuttled wide of the corpses, as though the sea itself had warned them off.

Kellan drank until he vomited into the sand, swearing between dry heaves that the boy had done it. Holt sharpened his blade with frantic rhythm, sparks spitting against stone. Garrick sat hunched, rocking, muttering fragments of prayer through his ruined nose.

Toby Cray sat apart from them all. The firelight painted his thin face in gold and shadow. He held the tome tight against his chest, rocking slightly, almost mirroring Garrick. To anyone watching, he looked like a rat hoarding stolen bread. But inside, beneath his ribs, he felt the tide of another heartbeat, slow and endless.

"You are mine."

The voice never stopped now. It curled into his thoughts as naturally as breath. It did not shout. It did not rage. It simply *was* the constant undertow beneath every sound.

At dawn, the first fight broke out.

Holt accused Kellan of bringing the curse by stealing from Redgrave's cave years ago — a necklace of black pearls that had since gone missing. Kellan lunged, knife flashing. The others pulled them apart, but not before blood slicked the sand.

By midday, half the camp carried cuts from half-hearted brawls. The rum was gone, thrown into the sea after one man claimed it smelled of rot. Hunger gnawed at them. The gulls' screams never stopped.

And always, the corpses on the shore stared with eyeless sockets, water swelling and draining from their slack mouths as if they still breathed with the tide.

That night, three men vanished.

No screams. No struggle. They were there by the fire one moment, and gone the next, their places empty as if the shadows had simply swallowed them whole.

The remaining crew searched the huts, the jungle, the beach. They found only wet footprints pressed into the sand, leading not away from camp, but *toward it.*

Toward Toby.

"Enough."

Kellan seized him by the collar, dragging him into the firelight. His scarred lip twisted into a snarl. "You're the source. You've been feeding us to the dead, one by one."

Toby struggled, clutching the book against his chest. "I didn't..."

"You stink of him!" Kellan roared, spittle flying. "Redgrave's rot drips off ye! I say we put him in the sea and be done."

The others shouted in agreement, fear hardening into violence. Even Garrick nodded, his ruined face glistening with sweat.

Toby's pulse raced. The firelight blurred. He could smell the brine of the pool though he was nowhere near the cave. His lips trembled, but the words that came from him were not his own.

"Touch me, and you'll rot with them."

The voice was deeper, sharper — Redgrave's voice spilling from Toby's throat. The crew froze. Their blades wavered.

Then came the sound.

The surf roared though the tide was low. Water rushed into camp, spilling between the huts, drenching the fire until it hissed and died.

From the foam rose shapes. Pale figures, seaweed dripping from their shoulders, barnacles bursting from their arms. Their jaws hung open, choking on brine, but their eyes were fixed and gleaming.

The drowned.

The men screamed. Knives and pistols flashed, but steel cut nothing but water. The drowned hands closed around wrists and ankles, pulling, dragging. One man fired his pistol point-blank into a hollow chest, the drowned staggered but did not fall. Another screamed as fingers hooked into his mouth and tore him backward into the surf.

The camp became chaos.

Toby fell to his knees in the water, clutching the tome. He should have been afraid. He should have run. But he felt calm.

Because they did not touch him.

The drowned surged past him, their hands brushing his shoulders, their hair whipping against his face, their mouths spilling water over him — but none laid claim to him. He was not prey.

He was chosen.

By dawn, silence fell again.

The camp was half-empty. Huts stood torn and waterlogged. The firepit was drowned in salt and sand.

Those who remained stared hollow-eyed at Toby, huddled in small knots, too afraid to sleep, too afraid to speak.

And on the beach, four more bodies had appeared.

Kellan. Garrick. Holt. And another who had not even fought, all of them sprawled in grotesque decay, as if they had been rotting in the sea for years. Barnacles split their skin, crabs scuttled through their ribs, and their mouths hung open to the sky as though they were still screaming.

Toby hugged the tome to his chest, shivering. His lips trembled, but when he finally whispered, it was not fear.

"Captain... I did what you asked."

Deep in the mountain, Redgrave's rotted body quivered against the nails.

The drowned had answered. The boy had bent. The crew had begun to crumble.

"Yes," he murmured, his ruined lips stretching wide, his one glowing eye fixed on nothing and everything. *"Yes, my Toby. Let them fall. Let their blood soak the sand. Each life binds you closer to me. Each death loosens my chains."*

The black pool below him rippled, reaching up in tongues of water that lapped at his nailed feet. The iron groaned.

Redgrave threw back his head and laughed, a sound like the sea smashing stone.

"Soon the island will be mine again. And through you, boy, the horizon will open."

Chapter Nine: The Dragging Deep

The camp was a graveyard.

The huts sagged with seawater, canvas rotting and torn, smoke long since choked from the fire. The air reeked of brine and decay. Toby Cray moved among it all in silence, the tome pressed against his chest, his ribs aching from the weight of its heartbeat.

He had not slept. His body shook with exhaustion, yet the voice in his head would not allow rest. Redgrave's whispers filled the silence, steady as the tide.

"They are gone. The island is yours now, Toby. My chosen. My vessel."

But the island was not empty.

The corpses of the drowned remained.

Kellan, Garrick, Holt, Vane, and the others, all sprawled where the surf had left them, their skin bloated, their sockets dark, their jaws gaping skyward. The gulls refused them. The crabs scuttled wide. Yet Toby could not look away.

Because he thought he saw one move.

It began with Vane.

His body lay half-buried in wet sand, barnacles clustering across his tattooed jaw. For hours he had been still, stiff as driftwood. But as Toby watched, his chest shuddered. A bubble of seawater escaped his lips.

The boy stumbled back, heart hammering.

Vane's arm twitched, fingers clawing weakly at the sand. His mouth worked, opening and closing, gurgling salt and brine. His eyes were still empty sockets, but his head turned, ever so slightly, toward Toby.

"...ra—t..."

The word scraped out raw, strangled, as if his throat were filled with glass.

Toby clutched the tome tighter, gasping.

Behind him, Garrick's corpse stirred. A wet, rattling breath hissed through the hole where his nose had once been. Holt's yellowed eyes cracked open, the pupils filmed over but fixed on Toby with dreadful focus.

The corpses were not alive. Not fully. But they were *returning*. Slowly, stiffly, as though the curse was knitting their broken forms back together with seawater and spite.

Toby staggered into the trees, his breath ragged. He pressed his back to a trunk, hugging the tome until his ribs hurt.

"What... what are they?" he whispered. His voice cracked with the sound of a child.

The captain's answer came smooth, low, patient.

"They are mine. They are what waits for those who deny me. And they are what you will command if you remain at my side."

"They're dead," Toby whimpered.

"Dead, and yet not. Do you see, Toby? Not even the sea can claim them. They serve me still."

Toby squeezed his eyes shut. He wanted to block out the image of Vane's twitching fingers, Garrick's rattling breath, Holt's blind stare. He wanted to throw the book away, to run, to vanish into the jungle.

But when his hands trembled, they did not release the tome. They clung tighter.

Because the truth clawed at him: the drowned had not touched him. They had dragged away the others, but *not him.* They had left him alone because he carried the captain's will.

For the first time in his life, Toby was untouchable.

By nightfall, the remaining men huddled together, too terrified to separate. They lit no fire. Fire drew the drowned.

They whispered among themselves, voices brittle.

"Did you see them move?" one hissed. "Their jaws, their hands..."

"They're not dead," another spat. "Not proper. Not natural."

"It's the boy. It's him. He's feeding them."

They cast glances at Toby, who sat alone at the edge of camp, the tome clutched in his lap. He looked half-dead himself, pale and sunken, his eyes wide and sleepless. But when one man drew too near, the air grew damp, and the sand beneath his boots filled with seawater. He backed away quickly.

No one dared touch him.

The next morning, Toby crept to the water's edge. He had not meant to. His feet carried him there without thought, drawn by a pull deeper than hunger.

The drowned waited.

Vane lay in the foam, chest rising shallowly, water spilling from his lips with every breath. His tattooed jaw had cracked, splitting open to reveal barnacles sprouting inside. Garrick twitched beside him, his ruined nose bubbling salt with every rasp. Holt crawled weakly, dragging his half-decayed body closer to the surf, as though the water itself summoned him back.

Their movements were slow, stiff, unnatural. Yet they were movements. They were *returning*.

And all of them, every twitching limb, every blind eye, strained toward Toby.

He stepped back, clutching the tome. His heart raced, but another sound filled him: the captain's laugh, low and terrible, echoing inside his ribs.

"Do you see, Toby? Do you see the strength I give? Death cannot end them. The tide raises them, just as it will raise you."

Deep in the cave, Captain Silas Redgrave stirred against the nails. His rotted head tilted, his one glowing eye gleaming as though it gazed through Toby's gaze, through the corpses on the shore.

"The drowned remember," he whispered, lips splitting in a ruined smile. *"And soon, they will rise to follow. As will you, my vessel. Through you, I will walk beyond this island. Through you, I will breathe salt into the lungs of the world."*

The nails creaked. Rust flaked. The black pool rippled, hungry.

And far down the beach, Toby Cray stood alone, the dead stirring at his feet, the tome clutched like a heartbeat in his chest.

Chapter Ten: The Vessel

The boy no longer dreamed his own dreams. When Toby Cray closed his eyes, he stood on a ship that did not exist, a vessel of black wood and iron nails, its sails ragged with seaweed, its timbers creaking with drowned breath. A shadow crew manned the ropes, their faces bloated, their sockets empty. At the helm, Captain Silas Redgrave steered through a sea as black as ink, his glowing eye fixed always on the horizon.

And always, at the captain's side, stood Toby, the tome pressed against his chest like a captain's log.

"You are mine," Redgrave whispered in every dream, his hand heavy and cold upon the boy's shoulder. "You are my voice, my hands, my tide. Through you, I will break my chains."

Toby woke shivering on the beach. The sun was pale, filtered through fog that never lifted. His stomach was a hollow pit, his throat raw with thirst, but none of it mattered anymore. He rose, clutching the tome.

The remaining pirates watched him with hollow eyes. Their camp had dwindled to less than a dozen men, and each one looked half-mad from hunger and fear. No one dared raise a hand against him now. They whispered instead, spitting curses when they thought he could not hear.

"Devil's   child."
"Witch's   rat."
"Redgrave's shadow."

He ignored them. Because when he moved, he did not move alone.

The drowned were rising.

Vane lay sprawled on the sand, chest heaving with a grotesque rhythm. Barnacles split open along his arms, spilling brine. His tattooed jaw gaped, and a wheezing groan bubbled up from the salt in his lungs.

Beside him, Garrick twitched and jerked, limbs stiff as driftwood. His ruined nose whistled with every rattling breath, though no air truly filled him. Holt crawled further from the surf each day, dragging himself inch by inch with clawing fingers, leaving furrows in the sand.

They were slow, pitiful, broken things. But each sunrise brought them further back. Their movements less stiff. Their groans more like words.

And always, their eyeless gaze turned toward Toby.

That night, Toby crept again to the cave. His body was frail, barely more than skin and bone, but the tome throbbed with warmth against him, filling him with strength that was not his own.

The black pool stirred at his arrival. Redgrave's nailed body sagged against the wall, but his head lifted when Toby entered, his mouth splitting in a ruined smile.

"You return, my Toby," the captain rasped.

"I don't have anywhere else to go," Toby whispered. His voice cracked, but his eyes no longer looked away. "They hate me. They fear me. Only you... only you call me by name."

Redgrave's laugh was a hollow thunder, rattling through the cavern.

"You are more than a name, boy. You are my vessel. The drowned answer to you because you carry my heart against your chest. The book is mine, and now it is yours. Do you see what that means?"

Toby swallowed hard. "That... I can command them?"

"That you are *me*," Redgrave hissed. His one glowing eye burned brighter, filling the cavern with its sickly light. "Speak, and they will move. Point, and they will kill. You will be my captain in flesh, until I walk free to wear my own skin again."

Toby's breath shuddered. He wanted to deny it. He wanted to scream. But his hands stroked the tome like a child with a comfort-blanket, and his lips parted to whisper the words he knew Redgrave wanted.

"...yes, Captain."

When Toby returned to camp, the men confronted him.

One of them, a young cutthroat named Brek, charged with a blade, spitting curses, swearing to gut the "witch boy" before the island claimed them all.

Toby flinched, but his voice came without thought, carried on the tide of Redgrave's will.

"Take him."

The drowned moved.

Vane lurched from the surf, staggering forward on stiff legs, his bloated chest wheezing. Garrick's ruined mouth whistled salt as he clawed into the camp. Holt dragged his bloated body behind them, his hands clawing deep grooves in the sand.

Brek froze. His knife trembled. Then he screamed as barnacled hands seized his arms, his legs, his jaw. The drowned pulled him into the tide, his shrieks choked to gurgles, then silence.

The remaining pirates backed away in horror, eyes wide, faces pale.

And Toby stood among them, the tome pressed tight against his chest, his voice cold.

"You see?" he said. His words cracked, his body shook, but the drowned loomed behind him, and his voice was not his own. "You can't touch me. You can't touch *us.*"

In the cave, Redgrave's nailed wrists quivered. Rust flaked from the spikes. His ruined head tilted back in laughter, wet and ragged.

"My vessel," he crooned. "My voice in the world. Every step you take loosens my bonds. Every command you give is a nail drawn free."

The pool surged beneath him, rising higher. Water lapped at his ribs, black and hungry.

"Serve me well, Toby," Redgrave whispered, his voice seeping into the boy's marrow across the island. "And when the island breaks, we shall sail again. You as my breath. I as your bones. Together, we will drown the world."

And in the camp, as the drowned clustered around Toby Cray, their jaws spilling brine, their bodies stiff but stirring, the boy lowered his head and whispered back:

"Yes, Captain."

Chapter Eleven: Ink and Skin

Long before the mutiny, long before the nails and the black pool, Captain Silas Redgrave stood alone in the hold of his ship.

The lantern-light swayed with the tide, casting gold across bloodstained planks. The stench of iron and brine hung heavy. Spread across the table before him lay the makings of his greatest work, parchment made not from animal hide but from flayed skin, stitched together with black sinew. A quill sharpened from bone. An inkpot filled with blood thickened by salt and ash.

Redgrave's hands moved with ruthless purpose. His coat was stripped off, sleeves rolled, revealing arms scored with scars, some new and bleeding. He dipped the quill, and with each stroke, his lips moved. Not in English. Not in any tongue men of flesh were meant to know.

The ship itself seemed to lean from his words. Lantern flames bent toward him. The air thickened, damp as though the sea had climbed into the hull.

From the shadows of the doorway, one man watched.

Rigg, a young sailor, pressed himself against the beams, terror choking his breath. He had followed his captain to this place, curious why Redgrave forbade them entry to the hold. What he saw now froze him in silence.

Redgrave's voice deepened with each line of script. His own blood dripped from fresh cuts along his arm, feeding the ink. The words crawled across the page as though alive, writhing with a pulse of their own.

Rigg stifled a gasp. The parchment, the *skin*, shuddered. For a heartbeat, a face appeared in its stretched surface, a mouth opening in silent scream before sinking back into stillness.

"Captain..." Rigg whispered before he could stop himself.

Redgrave's head snapped up. His eyes gleamed green, lantern-bright, burning with hunger.

"You shouldn't be here, boy." His voice was low, heavy, carrying the weight of tide and storm. "But since you are, you will *witness*. You will remember the night your captain broke the sea."

He dipped the quill again and scrawled faster, his words now bellowed. The blood-ink hissed, searing the parchment until smoke curled from it. The air vibrated, the timbers creaked, and water dripped from the beams though no leak broke them.

Rigg stumbled back, horror widening his eyes. "This, this is witchcraft!"

Redgrave smiled, his teeth black with blood. "No, lad. This is eternity."

The cave groaned with Redgrave's laughter.

Centuries had passed since that night in the hold, but the memory clung to him as vividly as the salt in his rotting veins. His tome still pulsed, his words still writhed. The boy clutched it to his chest as though it were a lifeline, never knowing it had been crafted from the very flesh of those who had once called Redgrave captain.

And now, through the boy, through Toby Cray, the work was nearly finished.

The nails that bound him to the wall were loosening. With each death, with each drowned sailor risen, with each command given in his name, the iron groaned. Rust bled into the pool below, flakes drifting like red snow across the black water.

Redgrave lifted his ruined head, his glowing eye fixed on the cavern's mouth.

"Freedom."

The word rattled out between his teeth, dripping rot. He could taste it. Not yet, but close. Closer than ever.

Through Toby's chest he felt the tome's heartbeat, echoing his own. Through the drowned he felt the tide filling their lungs, dragging their stiff limbs into motion again. Through the fear of the living pirates, he fed.

All of it led to one thing.

The horizon.

The pool surged, lapping higher, hungrier, as if eager to climb his nailed body. The drowned groaned outside, their voices rising into a chorus that shook the stone.

And in the camp, Toby Cray clutched the tome, trembling but unyielding, as Redgrave's whispers carved deeper into his marrow.

The captain's grin split wide, his jaw creaking.

"The last nail is loosening, my Toby. Soon I will stand. Soon I will breathe salt into the world once more. And you..."

His voice filled the cavern, his laughter spilling with it.

"You will be my keel. My rudder. My vessel. And when I sail again, all the oceans will drown at my command."

Chapter Twelve: The Vessel Breaks

The boy could not tell where his thoughts ended, and Redgrave's began.

At times, he remembered hunger, loneliness, the sting of fists, the laughter that named him "rat." At other times, he remembered blood rituals in the hold of a ship he had never sailed, runes carved into skin, the tide answering a dead man's voice. Both belonged to him. Both were true.

Toby Cray sat at the edge of the pool, the tome clutched tight and wept without sound. His tears dropped into the black water, rippling out toward the nailed figure on the wall.

"Do not cry, Toby."

The voice filled the cave, steady and patient, never cruel, never mocking. Redgrave's ruined head tilted forward, his glowing eye fixed upon the boy.

"You are no rat. You are my chosen. My vessel. You are more than they ever let you be."

Toby swallowed hard, his voice raw. "But am I anything without you?"

Silence. For a heartbeat, the cave was still.

Then Redgrave laughed, wet and broken, echoing against stone.

"Without me, you are bones in the sand. With me, you are tide and storm. Which life do you choose, my Toby?"

The last pirates lingered, gaunt and haunted, watching Toby with eyes full of hate and fear. They whispered about killing him, but none dared draw near. When they looked at him, they saw the drowned standing behind his shoulders, stiff and patient, waiting for command.

At night, they dreamed of water filling their lungs. At dawn, they woke with salt crusted on their lips.

One man broke finally, lunging at Toby with a knife. Toby cried out, raising the tome like a shield.

And the drowned answered.

Hands broke from the sand, dragging the attacker down. His screams curdled, cut short by brine. When the tide receded, another corpse lay stiff and barnacled beside the rest.

Toby shook, clutching the book, staring at the drowned clustered around him like guardians.

He whispered to the corpse on the wall, "I didn't mean..."

But the captain's voice thundered in his skull: *"Yes, you did."*

Days bled together. The surviving crew dwindled. The drowned multiplied. The island grew silent but for the gulls and the whispers of the mountain.

And Toby's heart withered.

He tried to remember his mother's face, but there was none. He tried to recall his father's voice, but there was only silence. He thought of his name, and it sounded foreign, useless. *Toby Cray.* A name that had brought him no safety, no love.

But when Redgrave said it, *"Toby,"* it carried weight. It carried belonging.

He began to whisper it back to himself, like a prayer.

Toby.

Chosen.

Vessel.

One night, when the fog pressed thick against the island and even the drowned were still, Toby crept deeper into the cave than he ever had before. The pool glistened like oil, and Redgrave's nailed body sagged heavy above it.

"Captain," Toby whispered, dropping to his knees. His voice cracked with both devotion and despair. "If I give you everything... will you keep me? Will I still be yours when you're free?"

The glowing eye burned brighter. The corpse smiled.

"Every vessel breaks, Toby. But not before it carries its master to shore."

The words gutted him. For a heartbeat, the boy's chest tightened with the scream of a child about to beg.

But then he looked at the water. At the drowned waiting beyond it. At the book pulsing in his hands.

And he knew there was no path left.

He bowed his head.

"Then let me carry you, Captain."

From the wall, Redgrave felt the last nail loosen in spirit, if not yet in steel.

The boy was gone now. The child had wept and broken, and what remained was vessel, body, mouthpiece. Through Toby's veins, the tide surged. Through Toby's trembling lips, his words spilled. Through Toby's devotion, his chains crumbled.

Soon the nails themselves would give way. Soon his feet would touch the black pool not as prisoner but as king returned.

He gazed down at the boy bowed before him, book pressed to his chest like a second heart.

"My Toby," Redgrave crooned, his voice rotting but full of triumph. *"My vessel. My tide. Carry me, and the world will drown at our feet."*

The pool stirred, swallowing the boy's reflection.

And Toby Cray, once a nameless rat, whispered back into the dark, without fear, without hesitation:

"Yes, Captain."

Chapter Thirteen: From the Shadows

The island was too quiet.

Harlan Briggs, once boatswain, once knife-fast and sea-tough, sat crouched behind the gutted remains of a hut, clutching a pistol with damp, shaking hands. His lips were cracked, his eyes bloodshot, his gut hollow with hunger. He had faced naval frigates, cannons, boarding parties. He had gutted men, robbed cities, burned villages. None of it haunted him like this cursed spit of rock.

The others were gone. Dragged beneath the surf, torn screaming into the fog, left rotting on the beach. Now only a handful of them remained, scattered like frightened gulls. He hadn't seen Toby Cray in a day, the little rat had vanished into the mountain, clutching that devil's book. And part of Harlan hoped the boy stayed there, far from the camp, far from *them*.

Because what was happening now had no name.

The corpses had stopped lying still.

Harlan's stomach turned as he watched from the tree line. Vane, aye, Vane, with his shark-toothed jaw tattoo, was moving. Not twitching, not gurgling, not crawling like a broken thing. Moving. His chest rose and fell with the rhythm of breath. His head rolled side to side as though he was loosening stiff neck muscles. His arms flexed, barnacles cracking and bursting from the joints.

And then, with a groan like timbers splitting, he sat up.

Harlan's breath caught. His pistol trembled. "No... no, Christ, no..."

Vane turned his head, slow as the tide, and fixed eyeless sockets on him.

And smiled.

Saltwater dripped from his ruined lips, teeth cracked and rimmed with barnacle flesh. His body sagged, but strength pulsed through it, a strength no corpse should bear.

Then Garrick stirred beside him. Holt dragged himself fully upright. Others followed. The drowned were *returning*. Not half-dead husks. Not twitching nightmares. Animated. Whole, in their own terrible way.

Harlan staggered back, choking on fear.

This was no curse of bad luck. This was no storm. This was *command*. Someone was calling them, binding them, filling their bloated chests with brine and will.

And Harlan knew who.

The rat-boy. The book. The captain nailed to the stone.

He ran.

Branches lashed his arms, his boots pounded the sand. He didn't know where he was going — only away. Away from the shore, from the drowned, from the eyeless sockets that still seemed to follow him even through the fog.

He stumbled, fell hard against stone, and realized too late where his panicked flight had carried him.

The cave.

The mountain's mouth yawned before him, jagged and wet, carved faces screaming from its walls. The air that wafted out was heavy with brine, thick with rot. His chest seized. His every instinct screamed to flee.

But a sound held him frozen.

Chains groaning. Nails straining. A voice like the tide filling his skull.

"Closer."

Harlan's pistol shook so badly he nearly dropped it. He backed away, eyes wide, breath ragged.

Something moved inside the dark.

Not the boy. Not the drowned. Bigger. Older. A shape that peeled itself from the wall where it had been bound for centuries. Rust screamed as iron strained. Barnacles cracked, falling into the black pool below.

A head lifted. One eye glowed faint, lantern-bright.

Silas Redgrave smiled through rotted teeth.

Harlan fired. The shot thundered in the cave, sparks flashing. Smoke filled his nostrils. When it cleared, the captain was still there, unmoved, smiling wider.

The shadows around him deepened. They spread across the walls, spilling toward Harlan like ink in water, crawling over the stone, swallowing torchlight, reaching for him with blackened hands.

Harlan screamed, stumbling back, pistol clattering uselessly into the dark. The shadows took his legs first, cold as the sea, dragging him down into the pool though he stood nowhere near it.

His last sight before the dark claimed him was Toby Cray, standing in the corner of the cavern, the tome clutched against his chest. The boy's face was pale, eyes wide, but he did not speak.

And Redgrave's voice thundered through the cave, filling every hollow, splitting every stone:

"One more nail, my Toby. One more, and I will walk again."

Harlan's scream was swallowed whole.

Chapter Fourteen: The Last Fire

The fire was almost gone.

A few embers glowed weakly in the sand, sputtering whenever the breeze carried salt from the sea. The pirates who remained, no more than four men, huddled around it as though it were the last sun in the world. Their eyes were hollow, their faces gray, their lips cracked with thirst. None spoke above a whisper. To speak louder was to invite the drowned.

And beyond the firelight, the drowned waited.

Their forms shambled on the shore, pale shapes rising with the tide, groaning with barnacled throats. Some dragged themselves across the sand, arms stiff but persistent. Others stood knee-deep in the water, swaying, as though listening for a command.

None came too close. Not yet.

The men stared at them until their eyes burned, until they could not tell if the shapes were moving or if their fear made the fog shift into phantoms.

Toby Cray did not sit with them.

He stood at the edge of camp, the tome clutched tight to his chest, watching the drowned as one might watch an army mustering for war. His clothes hung in tatters, his frame thin as driftwood, but there was no frailty in his gaze.

The whispers filled him always now. He no longer feared them. They were the tide, steady, endless. And he was its shore.

One of the men, a gaunt Spaniard with one eye, spat into the sand. "He's the devil's rat. Look at him. Standing there like he commands the corpses."

Another hissed back, "Not like. He *does.* Redgrave's ghost is in him."

Toby turned his head slowly. The men fell silent. His eyes were not glowing, not unnatural, but there was something in them that made their guts twist, a calm that no child beaten and starved should carry.

"You shouldn't speak of the captain," Toby said softly.

The Spaniard stiffened. "He *ain't* your captain."

"Yes," Toby whispered, his voice steady, unwavering. "He is."

The drowned stirred as the fog thickened.

Vane's bloated form no longer crawled — he walked. His tattooed jaw cracked when he moved, but his stride was steady. Garrick dragged his feet behind him, the whistle of his ruined nose wheezing with each breathless groan. Holt's body swayed, his head lolling, but his eyes, milky, filmed over, turned toward the campfire.

The surviving pirates saw them. Their courage broke.

"We can't stay here," one muttered, his voice shaking. "If we wait, they'll come for us. Better to risk the jungle. Better to..."

The words cut off as the surf hissed louder. Water sloshed across the sand, rushing further inland, licking the fire. The drowned groaned in unison, as if answering a single voice none of the living could hear.

The pirates scrambled back.

Toby did not move.

"Do you see, Toby?" Redgrave's voice pressed through his bones, louder than ever. *"They rise at my will, but they move at yours. You are my tide. You are my vessel. Tell them. Command them. Break the last of the crew, and my chains will snap."*

Toby's throat tightened. He stared at the fire, at the four broken men crouched behind it. Men who had beaten him, mocked him, spit on him. Men who had called him rat.

He could end them with a word.

He opened his mouth, then stopped.

"Captain," he whispered, so low the others could not hear. "When you're free... what happens to me?"

Silence. The only sound was the surf, the drowned groaning, the fire spitting its last sparks.

Then came the answer.

"Every vessel breaks, Toby. But not before it sails its master to shore."

The boy's eyes burned. A sob shuddered in his chest, but it never left his lips. He knew what it meant. He was never meant to live past this. He was a tool. A key. Nothing more.

But still, his hands clutched the tome tighter. Because to be used by Redgrave was still to be more than a rat. To be nothing was worse.

The drowned took another step.

The fire hissed out, drowned by the tide. Darkness swept the camp. The last pirates screamed, pistols flashing in the fog. Shots

cracked, sparks flew, but the drowned did not fall. They surged forward, their groans building into a low, endless chorus.

Toby closed his eyes. He pressed the tome to his chest and whispered, steady, resigned, devoted:

"Yes, Captain."

And the drowned obeyed.

In the cave, the nails groaned, splitting stone. Rust fell in showers. The black pool surged high, licking at his ribs. Redgrave's ruined head lifted, his glowing eye blazing brighter than it had in centuries.

"The last tide comes, my Toby. Soon I will stand."

His laughter thundered from the mountain, carrying across the island, shaking huts, rattling bones.

And in the camp, the screams of the last pirates were swallowed by the fog, until only the groans of the drowned and the whispers of the captain remained.

Chapter Fifteen: The Hollow Boy

The island was quiet again.

No gulls cried. No men cursed. No laughter, no singing, no drunken jeers. The camp was a graveyard of half-rotted huts and drowned corpses. The tide lapped at the sand in patient rhythm, as if mocking the silence it had left behind.

And Toby Cray sat alone by the black pool, the tome pressed against his knees.

His bones ached with exhaustion, his eyes hollow with sleepless nights, but he did not tremble anymore. His tears had dried. His fear had dulled. What filled him now was something colder, heavier.

Acceptance.

He stared into the water. It gave him no reflection. It never had. The pool swallowed light whole, offering back only emptiness. Yet when he looked long enough, he thought he saw shapes moving in its depth, figures with barnacled jaws and seaweed hair, eyes glowing faint. The drowned, waiting below.

He clutched the tome tighter.

"They'll never laugh at me again," he whispered. His voice was thin, hoarse from disuse. "They'll never call me rat. Never kick me into the dirt."

The words felt strange, like he was speaking into a void. He knew no one was listening. Not truly. Not except *him.*

"I hear you, Toby."

The captain's voice rolled through his chest, warm and patient, carrying weight like the tide.

Redgrave did not shout. He did not command. He only *was*, constant, unyielding, and endless.

"You were never rat. You were never nothing. You are my chosen vessel. My vessel. Through you, I will breathe again."

Toby closed his eyes. The words sank into him, filling every hollow the world had carved out of him.

"But when you're free..." His throat tightened. "What happens to me, Captain?"

For a moment, silence. Only the drip of water in the cave.

Then the captain spoke again, softer now.

"Every vessel breaks, Toby. But you will not break in vain. Your bones will be the keel. Your blood will be the tide. Through you, I will sail."

The boy's lip trembled. A shiver ran through him, not of fear but of grief. He had known the answer. He had always known. He was never meant to live past this.

But still, he hugged the tome tighter.

Because even as a vessel, he was more than he had ever been.

He thought of the nights in camp, lying curled in the sand while the men drank and mocked him. He thought of the fists, the kicks, and the jeers. He thought of how no one had ever said his name, how even the sound of it felt foreign until Redgrave had spoken it.

Toby.

The captain had said it as though it meant something. And that had been enough.

Toby Cray was no rat.
Toby Cray was chosen.
Toby Cray was the vessel.

The pool rippled. Chains groaned against stone. The nailed figure stirred above him, lifting its ruined head. One glowing eye fixed on Toby, burning brighter now, as though lit from within by the dawn itself.

"The time is near, my Toby."

The boy bowed his head. His voice was steady now, his lips dry but certain.

"I'm ready, Captain."

The tome pulsed in his hands, its pages twitching faintly like skin stretched over breath. The drowned groaned faintly in the distance, their voices rising with the tide.

And Toby Cray, hollow and trembling but no longer afraid, closed his eyes and whispered the only words that still belonged to him:

"Yes, Captain."

Chapter Sixteen: The Groaning Choir

We are not men. We are not gone.
We are tide.
We are weight.
We are the hunger of the sea given flesh.

The first breath burned. Salt tore through what lungs remained, swelling them, stiffening them, filling them with brine until they could no longer collapse. But we did not drown. We rose.

Hands, stiff and cracked, clawed from the surf. Jaws, swollen and barnacled, opened in groans that were not words but still carried meaning. We rose together, pulled by the voice in the deep, the one who had named us.

Captain.

His command throbbed through the tide, through the marrow of our bones, through the rot that clung to our skin. We heard him not with ears, but with what remained of us. His voice was the sea, and we were its echoes.

We remembered things, shards of lives that once were. Vane remembered the bite of rum, the sting of tattoos hammered into his jaw. Garrick remembered the laughter of mutiny, the sound of hammers striking nails. Holt remembered nothing but the blade that had taken his eye, the taste of iron and salt.

But these were dim, brittle. What was sharp and clear was the call.

The captain.

The boy.

The book.

Through the boy, we heard him. Through the boy, we moved. Through the boy, we served.

We shambled from the surf, barnacles splitting as we bent our stiffened limbs. Our eyes saw little, but we felt the heat of living men huddled in the camp, their hearts beating, their fear spilling into the sand. They smelled of salt and iron, prey in the captain's tide.

We lurched closer. Some fired pistols, some raised knives, but their strikes passed through us like splinters of foam. We groaned, we clutched, we pulled. Their screams fed the tide. Their blood fed the pool.

We did not eat. We did not drink. We only dragged them down, where the water could claim what breath remained.

The boy watched. He did not flinch. His small hands clutched the book as if it were his skin, his ribs, his very heart. We turned our hollow sockets toward him and felt the captain's will pulse through us.

Do not touch him.

We did not. We circled him instead, guardians of rot, a choir of drowned throats groaning his name without breath.

To-by. To-by. To-by.

In the cave, the captain shifted. The nails strained. The pool rippled. We felt his hunger in our bones, his laughter vibrating through the brine in our bellies.

One more. One more tide. One more vessel broken, and I will walk again.

We groaned as one, a chorus, a tide made flesh. We staggered in the fog, our jaws unhinging, our fingers splitting, our ribs snapping open as barnacles sprouted fresh. We were not men. We were not gone.

We were the captain's shadow, the proof of his will.

And when he rose, we would rise higher.

When he breathed, we would breathe again.

When he sailed, the world would drown.

Chapter Seventeen: The Breaking of Chains

The island groaned.

The mountain's heart throbbed like a drumbeat, deep and resonant, shaking stone and sand alike. The last survivors cowered in what remained of the camp, pistols trembling, knives slick with sweat. Their eyes were hollow, their lips cracked, their whispers little more than prayers to a God that had long since turned his face from this cursed place.

The drowned surrounded them in the fog, their chorus rising, a guttural chant that shook the air.

To-by. To-by. To-by.

And from the mouth of the cave, the boy stood.

Toby Cray, no longer a rat, no longer a child, held the tome against his chest, his hair plastered by salt, his eyes empty but certain. He looked toward the mountain, toward the black pool, toward the nailed figure that had called him.

"Captain," he whispered.

The earth split.

Inside the mountain, the pool surged. Black water spat against the walls, licking at the nailed corpse. Redgrave's ruined body quivered, rust shrieking as the spikes bent, splintering stone. Barnacles cracked. His head lifted, his one glowing eye burning brighter than fire.

The first nail tore free.

It clattered into the pool with a hiss, swallowed whole. The captain's left arm sagged, flesh tearing, bone creaking, but still he smiled.

The second nail screamed loose, shattering stone.

Chains rattled, iron splitting like driftwood. His right arm dropped, the joints stiff but trembling with new strength.

"Free..." Redgrave's voice rolled through the cave, through the camp, through the bones of every man alive or drowned. His laughter roared like surf on stone. "Free at last!"

The last nails tore free. His body fell forward into the pool with a thunderous splash. The water did not swallow him, it *rose to meet him*, surging upward, lifting him like a throne.

From the black tide he stood.

Captain Silas Redgrave, rotted, barnacled, eyes burning green, was free.

The survivors screamed. Some fled into the trees. Others fired pistols uselessly into the fog. The drowned surged forward, groaning with joy, their jaws snapping, their fingers clawing. The last men were dragged under, their cries strangled by salt.

Toby did not run. He did not scream. He stepped forward, closer to the cave, closer to the rising captain.

The tide reached for him. Hands of water, barnacled and pale, seized his legs, his arms, his chest. He gasped, clutching the tome tighter.

"Captain!"

The pool swallowed his cry.

The drowned ones' groaned louder, their chorus shattering the night. Redgrave's laughter echoed above it, rolling through stone and sand, through sky and tide.

The island shuddered, the mountain split, and the boy Toby Cray was dragged beneath the black water.

The captain stood tall above the pool, water cascading from his ruined body, barnacles bursting, seaweed streaming from his coat. His glowing eye burned through the fog, and his voice thundered like cannon fire.

"My chains are broken. My tide has risen. The world will drown!"

His arms spread wide, as though to embrace the horizon itself. The drowned ones roared with him, their groans becoming one terrible, endless chorus.

And in the pool below, Toby vanished.

The captain smiled, teeth splitting rotten lips.

"My vessel sails at last."

Chapter Eighteen: The First Mate

The water was endless.

It filled his mouth, his throat, his lungs. Salt burned his chest, but he did not choke. He sank through blackness, deeper and deeper, though there was no bottom. Shapes drifted around him, pale hands, eyeless faces, open mouths spilling sand and brine. The drowned swam beside him, their movements jerky and stiff, yet graceful in the current that bound them all.

He should have died.

But death did not come.

At first, Toby Cray tried to scream. His body convulsed, his chest heaved, but the black water did not let go. It pressed into him, filling every hollow, every vessel, until he could no longer tell where he ended and the tide began.

His eyes burned. His skin split. Barnacles cracked through his flesh, like teeth sprouting from bone. Saltwater poured from his veins, and he felt his blood carried away into the sea.

But with the pain came strength. His limbs grew heavy, powerful, as if the tide itself moved them. His chest no longer ached. His lungs no longer gasped. He did not breathe, he did not need to.

He opened his eyes.

The world glowed faintly green.

Through the current, through the endless black, a figure rose before him.

Captain Silas Redgrave.

He was taller now than Toby remembered, broader, a ruin of a man made whole by tide and rot. Barnacles crusted his arms, seaweed draped from his shoulders, and his glowing eye burned brighter than the lanterns of a hundred ships. He did not float, the water carried him, enthroned by the sea itself.

Around him, the drowned groaned their endless chant. They bent without bending, bowed without breath, their heads turning toward him like weeds drawn to the tide.

Redgrave smiled when he looked at Toby.

"My Toby."

The voice filled every part of him, vibrating through his marrow, his barnacles, his hollowed veins.

"You carried me. You broke my chains. And now you sail with me, as first among the drowned."

Toby opened his mouth. No air came. No words rose. Only brine. Yet the captain heard him.

He thought "*I am yours.*"

And Redgrave answered: *Yes. Forever.*

The other drowned closed in, surrounding him in their circle. Their eyeless sockets fixed on him, their groans rising into a chorus that shuddered through the sea. They touched him, cold, stiff hands brushing his shoulders, his face, his arms. They welcomed him. Not as prey. Not as rat.

As one of them.

As first among them.

Above, the island trembled. Waves slammed the shore harder than ever before. Trees bent and split. The last embers of fire hissed and died beneath the rising tide.

And still Toby drifted, his body no longer his own, his heart a barnacle-encrusted stone in his chest.

He should have felt sorrow. He should have wept for the boy he had been. But there was no grief now. Only calm. Only belonging.

He turned his eyes, pale, glowing faint like the rest, toward Redgrave, and in his chest a groan rose to match the others.

Together, the drowned sang beneath the waves, a groaning choir that shook the mountain itself.

And in the captain's burning eye, Toby saw the horizon.

Not just the island. Not just the black pool.

The world.

Far beyond the reach of suns or gravity, a void shard stirred.

Forged by the interference of a power older than creation, it slipped through the dark with one unwavering trajectory.

Earth.

Three calamities had risen in the earth, each unaware of the other, unaware that soon their tides, roots, and frost would crash together.

<u>Special Thanks</u>

This page and the following pages are dedicated to all those who helped contribute to this project. These stories have burned at the back of my mind for almost 15 years. Without these folks, this project would have sat in my notebook forever. Thank you all for your support and thank you for believing in the project and being a part of this journey.
My Wife
(Support)
My Son
(Helped with the Audiobook and Provided Some Artwork)
My Daughter
(provided Maniacal laughter)
Kelli Pledger
(BETA Reader)
Kaylee Gouge
(Character Illustrations)
Monty Anderson
(Cover Art)
Rebecca Engleman
(Contributing Artist and BETA reader)
Sara Findley
(BETA Reader)
Without these people I would not have pursued this, and these monsters would never be unleashed into the world. Be on the lookout for the next book. Sour Worlds: Conflict coming soon.

Author's Note

This book is not about heroes. It is about places that remember, forces that endure, and the consequences of being noticed by things older than us. The world in these pages are cruel not because they choose to be, but because cruelty is what remains when patience outlasts mercy.

Sour World: Calamities was written with the belief that horror works best when it is inevitable when resistance is possible, but survival was guaranteed. The forest does not hate. Hell does not rage. The sea does not rejoice. They simply *wait*. And eventually, someone listens.

The creatures within these stories were never meant to be monsters in the traditional sense. They are reflections of neglect, of arrogance, of despair, of the human need to belong to something larger than ourselves, even if it consumes us. The Knot does not conquer; it collects. The Harrow does not destroy; he continues. The drowned do not judge; they welcome.

Each part of this book explores a different kind of surrender: to silence,

to hunger,

to purpose,

to the lie that becoming something else will finally make the pain stop.

If there is a unifying truth beneath these stories, it is this: no place is empty, no structure is inert, and nothing built from borrowed bones is truly safe.

These words were not created quickly. They have been tightening in my mind for years, growing quietly, waiting for their turn to be told. Once written, they refuse to stay contained. And now they belong to you as much as they ever did to me.

Read carefully.

Listen closely.

And if a voice answers back from these pages,

don't answer it.

--Jaymes Bishop--

A note on the Series

Sour Worlds: Calamities is not a self-contained story.

It is the opening movement in a larger collapse. The events in this book do not resolve the world's fate, the destabilize it. What follows is not a linear struggle toward victory, but an escalation of incompatible truths. The frost spreads because it believes it must. The tide advances because it has learned a way forward. The forest grows because reclaiming the world was never a choice.

Each force acts according to its own internal logic. None of them are wrong. None of them are merciful.

AS the series continues, boundaries will erode between worlds, between identities, between what is alive and what has merely learned to persist. Alliances will not form cleanly. Survival will not look like triumph. And silence will begin to matter more than conquest.

There was never a way back...

The consequences are permanent.

And the world will not emerge unchanged, regardless of who remains standing.

About the Author

Jaymes Bishop is a horror author and world-builder from Arkansas, best known for creating the expanding dark fiction universe known as the Sour Worlds. His stories blend supernatural horror, folklore, and cosmic dread, often set against the shadowy forests and forgotten places of rural America.

Jaymes began developing the mythology behind the Sour Worlds more than a decade ago, crafting interconnected stories filled with unsettling entities, fractured realities, and the fragile line between the natural world and the unknown. His work is inspired by classic horror influences such as Scary Stories to Tell in the Dark, Goosebumps, and the atmospheric storytelling of Stephen King.

His debut book, Sour Worlds: Calamities, introduces readers to the origins of the strange forces that haunt the series' universe where ancient powers stir, unseen observers watch from beyond reality, and ordinary people find themselves caught in events far larger than they understand.

When he isn't writing, Jaymes spends time with his family creating memories.

www.ingramcontent.com/pod-product-compliance
Lightning Source LLC
Chambersburg PA
CBHW020325160726
47992CB00004B/1700